OBERO

"Oberon is the best dog in modern fantasy, and learning fascinating bits of history alongside him is an absolute delight. Iron Druid fans will lap this collection up, but it's also a perfect way to step into Kevin Hearne's enchanting world for the first time."
—Greg van Eekhout, author of *California Bones* and *Voyage of the Dogs*

"Like a great sausage, there's a bit of everything in here and a few lovely surprises, too!"
—Jason M. Hough, *New York Times* bestselling author of *The Darwin Elevator*

"Wisdom, compassion, adventure, and canine Zen, paw-delivered one beefy bacon sausage cheesy truth at a time. The perfect read for every mood."
—K.C Alexander, author of *Necrotech*

PRAISE FOR

THE IRON DRUID CHRONICLES

"Hearne, a self-professed comic-book nerd, has turned his love of awesome dudes whacking mightily at evil villains into a superb urban fantasy debut. Atticus and his trusty sidekick, Irish wolfhound Oberon, make an eminently readable daring duo with plenty of quips and zap-pow-bang fighting."
—*Publisher's Weekly,* starred review

"Kevin Hearne breathes new life into old myths, creating a world both eerily familiar and startlingly original."
—Nicole Peeler, author of *Tempest Rising*

PRAISE FOR

INK & SIGIL

"Immensely enjoyable...Ink & Sigil is a great entry into Kevin Hearne's fiction...a great novel and a perfect example of how to launch a new series."
—*SFFWorld*

"Goodness, this book was funny, so funny. What a unique, entertaining and complex protagonist."
—*The BiblioSanctum*

"A terrific kick-off of a new, action-packed, enchantingly fun series . . . delightful."
—*Booklist (starred review)*

"A refreshing viewpoint into an urban fantasy setting [with] touches of humor and dynamic characters . . . Readers will be eager to see what happens next."
—*Publishers Weekly*

"Delightful! Hearne's use of Scottish words and spellings . . . adds to the story's singular flavor. The author includes plenty of shout-outs for fans of the "Iron Druid" series [in this] tale sure to draw in new readers."
—*Library Journal*

PRAISE FOR

THE SEVEN KENNINGS

"You'll laugh and cry and crave mustard as you're immersed in the literal magic of storytelling in Kevin Hearne's vivid new epic fantasy. I have experienced acute withdrawal symptoms since the book ended. I don't want to leave this world."
—Beth Cato, author of *A Thousand Recipes for Revenge*

"*A Plague of Giants* is an absorbing epic fantasy, with clever storytelling that allows its many threads to each feel important, personal, and memorable. I'm very much looking forward to the sequel!"
—James Islington, author of *The Shadow of What Was Lost*

OBERON'S BATHTIME STORIES

OTHER WORKS BY KEVIN HEARNE

THE IRON DRUID CHRONICLES
Hounded *Hunted*
Hexed *Shattered*
Hammered *Staked*
Tricked *Besieged*
Trapped *Scourged*

INK & SIGIL
Ink & Sigil
Paper & Blood
Candle & Crow

THE SEVEN KENNINGS
A Plague of Giants
A Blight of Blackwings
A Curse of Krakens

THE TALES OF PELL
CO-AUTHORED WITH DELILAH S. DAWSON
Kill the Farm Boy
No Country for Old Gnomes
The Princess Beard

OBERON'S MEATY MYSTERIES
The Purloined Poodle
The Squirrel on the Train
The Buzz Kill (in Death & Honey)
The Chartreuse Chanteuse (in Canines & Cocktails)

SCIENCE FICTION
The Hermit Next Door
A Question of Navigation

OBERON'S BATHTIME STORIES

KEVIN HEARNE

Horned Lark Press

This is a work of fiction. All of the characters, organizations, and events portrayed in these stories are either products of the author's imagination or are used fictitiously.

Tacos are the best idea ever, though. That's nonfiction.

OBERON'S BATHTIME STORIES

Oberon's Bathtime Stories Copyright © 2025 by Kevin Hearne

Cover Art Copyright © 2025 by Phineas X. Jones

All rights reserved. No part of this book may be reproduced or distributed without permission from the author or publisher. No part of this book may be used in any manner for the purpose of training large language model systems or any other artificial intelligence technologies.

A Horned Lark Press Book

Published by Horned Lark Press
1087-2482 Yonge Street
Toronto, ON M4P 2H5

www.hornedlarkpress.com

2 4 6 8 9 7 5 3 1

First Edition

Print ISBN: 978-1-998390-15-1
Ebook ISBN: 978-1-998390-16-8

Printed in a Secret Volcano Lair by Antifascist Capybaras

For People Who Love Dogs

STORIES (BUBBLES NOT INCLUDED)

The Watchmaker	1
The Grocery Sack of Rome	13
Another Mountain to Climb	24
The Human Dynamo	33
The Triple Nonfat Double Bacon Five-Cheese Mocha	43
The Spy Who Wrote Plays	60
Mississippi Devil	69
The Thinker	79
The Skinny Dipper	89
Seeking Harmony	100
A Riotous Distraction	109
The Man Who Dodged the Guillotine	119

THE WATCHMAKER

Listen: There are no downsides to playing with wombats. They are roly-poly and like to horse around so long as they know you don't want to eat them. And when you have a Druid who can let them know you just want to play, they are the friendliest, roundest little dudes who tumble and spin and occasionally bruise me with their weaponized butts.

They're not weaponized the way you're thinking: I'm not talking about gas attacks. They have four fused bony plates in their butts and if they catch you just right with a spin move, it can really hurt. But I like a soupçon of danger. (A soupçon means *a little bit* and it reminds me that I wouldn't say no to a little bit of soup or maybe some bone broth if you have any, so it's one of my favorite words now. If you don't understand why a little bit of soup is just the best thing, that's because you don't lick it up like hounds do and have it soak into your beard hair under your lips so you can keep tasting it for days. A soupçon of soup goes a long way, and if you can grow a beard to savor flavors long after the food is gone, I highly recommend it. Atticus will never admit it, but that little patch of chin fur he grows is a flavor saver that he savors whenever he thinks I'm not looking.)

My Boston terrier buddy, Starbuck, loves wombats too. We play with them all the time, now that we live in Tasmania.

But even though they're round, a fun fact about wombats is that they poop in cubes. They are the only animal in the world that does. At first, I was in awe of the craftsmanship displayed by their large intestines, because I can't teach mine to do anything, let alone sculpt poop into shapes, but Atticus explained that this had something to do with the musculature of their colons and was not something they did consciously.

"They do, however, leave cubes on rocks and roots and things around their territory to communicate with other wombats."

<Communicate?> I said, using the mental link I had with Atticus. <Is this where the phrase "shit talking" comes from?>

"No. Well, maybe? It's unlikely, but I'm not sure. The origin of slang can be surprising. I should make that one my next research project."

He got out his phone and started to tap out a search with his thumb, and that was my cue to keep playing with the wombats. Starbuck and I were playing with a couple of them in the forested hills near Launceston. We were very close, in fact, to the spot where we found a dead guy under a feral beehive, where Atticus first met Rose.

Atticus had been helping Tasmanian devils recover from a contagious face cancer at the time, but he'd worked that out and stabilized the population. He had other projects to work on now for various elementals around the world.

My wombat playmate spun a couple of times, whipping that dangerous butt around, and I had to leap back to avoid it and I barked at him so he would feel good about getting a big guy like me on the ropes. But on my third leap back I tripped on a branch or something and actually fell over, and when I rolled to keep out of range I felt something go kinda squishy under my side and I smelled it when I got to my feet: some other kind of animal poop, now matted in my fur.

You might be thinking, "Hey! Now that's a downside to playing with wombats!" but no, it was all good. Because it meant I was going to get a bath when I got home, and whenever I get a bath, I get a story from Atticus. Stories from Atticus are the best because you never know if it's going to be an adventure or a romance or a mystery or a philosophical thing. But it always gives me something to think about afterward, and I like that part just as much—if not more—than the story itself.

So like I said: wombats are rad.

After we said goodbye to them and went home, Atticus told me to go straight to the bathroom and hop in the tub, because I was not allowed to stink up the house with some random animal's feces.

Atticus hosed me down with an attachment to the tub faucet thingie to get the worst of it off, which was kind of noisy because water pressure is like that, but then he grabbed a giant squeezy bottle of soap and asked if I was ready.

<Ready for soap and a story, aye aye!>

He squeezed the bottle all over my coat and then went to work on scrubbing me, and while he did that, he told me a story.

Back in the twentieth century, people didn't look at their phones to see what time it was. They looked at their watches, either worn on their wrist or kept in their pocket, though they might also look at clocks on the wall or on bedside tables. Timepieces were both functional and aesthetic, and if cared for, they were heirlooms passed down through generations. I myself have owned many wonderful watches, and sometimes I miss the precision of the ticks and tocks–an altogether different meaning than TikTok today.

Since most people had watches and since they sometimes needed repair, it was possible back then to make a living as a watchmaker. They might *repair* watches more often than make new ones, but even if their entire living was based on repair, they were still called watchmakers.

During World War II there was a watchmaker in Haarlem–I mean the city outside of Amsterdam, not the Harlem outside of New York–called Ten Boom Watches.

<Ten Boom? Like ten explosions?>

"No, *boom* means *tree* in the Dutch language."

<It does? Then what does *boomshakalaka* mean in Dutch? Tree shaking? Or maybe tree sausage? Hey, is this secretly a story about sausage?>

"No, it means nothing in Dutch. *Boomshakalaka* is an American slang term popularized by a movie called *Stripes* and then later, a video game about basketball. It's an exclamation used to express triumph and dominance."

<Whoa. Slang origins *can* be surprising. But I already knew what it meant, Atticus. Remember how you used to cast camouflage on me so I could sneak up and scare Mrs. MacDonagh's cats to measure their vertical leap? Granuaile did that for me once somewhere else and she said "Boomshakalaka!" when the cat hit the ceiling and that's where I learned it.>

"When was this?" Atticus frowned at me.

<It was that time—I mean, I just remembered that I'm not supposed to remember that, it never happened. Oh! It must have been a dream! Yeah! I just like to dream about cats hitting the ceiling, I'd never really try to make that happen, because it was an accident, that thing that...didn't happen.>*

"I don't believe you, but you can keep it a secret if you want. Anyway, Ten Boom was just the Dutch surname of the family that owned the watchmaker shop."

<Ah, okay. Sorry to interrupt. Please continue.>

During World War II, I heard of this shop in Haarlem because I was helping some people that the Ten Booms had also helped earlier on. I was living in the French Pyrenees, guiding people over them to Spain and thence to Portugal where they could catch a boat to England or America. These people were Jewish families trying to escape the Nazis, and they wound up in my care after journeying from many different countries in Europe. I was just one part of the resistance helping them escape, a network that hid and shielded and guided families who needed it. The Ten Booms were another part of that network, and I heard about them from a family who had spent some time in their care.

Normally a family fleeing the Netherlands would not make it to me—they'd have to cross all of France from north to south, and that made little sense when they could just sail across the channel to England. But the Nazis were swarming the area with their navy and air force, and ships were not always reliable. Through a series of mishaps and the need to avoid Nazis and keep moving, this family kept heading south and was eventually given to my care. And during our journey across the Pyrenees, they told me about the Ten Booms.

There was Casper, the father; Willem, the son; and three daughters, Corrie, Betsie, and Nollie. They lived above the watch shop, and in Corrie's room, they had modified the wall to create a narrow space where up to six people could hide if necessary. This family had found it necessary. They stayed with the Ten Booms for three days, and had to use that secret space on one occasion when the Nazis came calling.

That family made it to the States, eventually, though one of them got sick on the long ride across the Atlantic and never fully recovered. But they were just a few of approximately eight hundred people that the Ten Booms saved. And they did this at great personal risk for two years. But eventually, in 1944, they got caught. Someone ratted them out, and they were arrested, except for Nollie, who was not present at the time.

They were taken to prisons in Germany—work camps, really, that the Nazis had set up—and there Casper and Betsie died. Willem contracted tuberculosis in prison and passed away not long after the war. But Corrie Ten Boom survived to old age. She wrote a book about her family's experience called *The Hiding Place*.

And I guess I'm telling you about them because I admire how they quietly worked to fight against evil the only way they knew how. They weren't warriors; they were watchmakers. But they saw people who needed help and they gave it. They could not defeat the evil outright, but they denied it victory. They saved what lives they could, when they could have chosen to do nothing.

Atticus abruptly stopped there, though he kept scrubbing me a bit in a sort of absent-minded circle. The bubbles tickled and I wanted to shake myself so badly, but I knew it wasn't time yet. I was thinking about how often I chose to do nothing. For me it's often a great choice—have you ever heard of naps? They're amazing! But if you have a chance to save someone's life, of course, you don't sleep on that.

<Why did the Ten Booms do it, Atticus? Were they brave?>

"I think they *were* brave, yes, but that's not a reason for them to do something so dangerous."

<Then why did they do it, if it was so dangerous? Most of them died, right?>

"I can't know for sure since I never met them. It would be speculation."

<Can I have a soupçon of speculation, then?>

"I think maybe it had something to do with time. As watchmakers they were intensely aware of it—how it never stops moving, but also its cyclical nature, and how we only get so much of it measured out to us. What you do with the time you have is important. The Ten Booms wanted to spend their time helping people, and they did. And their motivation for helping most likely derived from their faith. They were Calvinists—a sect of Christianity that held that Jews were considered special in God's eyes. They never tried to convert any of the Jews to Christianity. They just helped."

He started to rinse me off and that tickled even more, but I held off on the shaking. He doesn't mind if I shake once the soap is gone. And I was distracted anyway by wondering why he chose to tell me this particular story. It was kind of short and featured heavy themes.

A lot of times, Atticus will choose a story that he knows will make me happy. Like that time he told me about Francis Bacon, or that other time he told me about the infinitely groovy dude, Wavy Gravy. A story where I get to learn all this stuff about an interesting person *and* think about food the whole time? Yes, please! But sometimes he tells me stories that have a lot more to do with what's on his mind. I think this was one of those times, because the people in the story didn't eat anything.

The Ten Booms were living through a wartime occupation and surrounded by bad guys, hopelessly outnumbered and very much outgunned in Haarlem. And Atticus is one of only three old-fashioned Druids in a world of billions of humans, all of them polluting the air and water and driving plant and animal species to extinction, and sometimes he feels overwhelmed at the task of protecting Gaia. I know that because he tells me. There's no way he can win. He's just trying to help as much as he can, like the Ten Booms. So maybe that was why he was thinking about them.

He declared me clean and I finally got to shake, showering the bathroom with water, and then I got a towel-down and another shake before I got out of the tub to get my feet dried off.

"Time for zoomies?" Atticus said.

<Aye, Cap'n, zoomies ahoy!>

He opened the bathroom door and I zoomed out of there, turning sharply a few times until I rocketed out of the extra-large doggie door they had installed at the back of Rose's house, where my little buddy Starbuck joined me for a nice ripping run around the backyard. He was going to get a bath next, so this was his last chance to get dirty while I was going to try to stay clean. He wiped out a couple of times on purpose, kind of the way football players do to see if they can get the ref to call a penalty, except he was just trying to get his coat full of dirt and grass and stuff before going into the tub. We take pride in leaving a ring of dirt in the bathtub after the water drains, and we think Atticus likes it too, because it gives him a sense of accomplishment.

<What was the story about?> Starbuck asked. <Was there any food?>

<I'm not going to spoil the surprise.>

We ran until we were panting and Starbuck was absolutely filthy, and Atticus called him in to get his bath. I went inside to lie down on my luxury doggie bed and have a nap, but I reevaluated the story before I drifted off.

Trying to help was only *part* of what Atticus was thinking about, I realized. The other part was about time, and how you decided to use what time you had.

Atticus has had a lot more time to live than most humans and he worries sometimes that he hasn't used the time wisely. I'm not very good with numbers past twenty, but he told me once that if humans lived a hundred years in their lifetime, then he had lived twenty lifetimes. And he told me recently that I've lived three or four wolfhound lifetimes now, so maybe I should worry if I'm using the time wisely too.

Worrying is not a great use of my time, though.

Zooming and playing and snuggling and napping and eating sausage with gravy, that's the way to live. I think I have that figured out. If I have a job, it's to remind Atticus of that.

He needs me around, you know. Atticus zones out sometimes, but in different ways. When he's communing with an elemental or even Gaia, his face looks serene and untroubled. I never bother him then, and I've trained Starbuck to recognize that too so Atticus can do his Druid things in peace. But if his eyes kind of go glassy and his expression looks haunted and haggard, then I have to act, because he's dwelling on his past and feeling guilt or regret and that's not good for him. (*Haggard* is a word that I associate with the actor Billy Bob Thornton in *Bad Santa*. If your human ever starts to look the way he did in that movie, intervention is required.)

Here is how you yank a human out of their haunted reverie and drag them back into the present: Stick your tongue in their ear.

And listen, do it right, okay? Don't just lap gently at their earlobe. Get all the way deep-off-up-in there and taste the earwax.

This is easier for me than humans but it still requires skill, because wolfhound tongues are designed to lap from the bottom up. If I just did that, however—a standard lick—I'd miss the canal. You have to stay on target and fire your tongue in there like it's a photon torpedo aimed at the small exhaust port on the Death Star. If you do that, I guarantee your human will mentally return to the here and now on the instant.

It is not without its danger, however. You have to be aware that you're taking a risk. The human might simply cringe away and say "Ew!" but there's a significant chance of unrestrained flailing and you could get whacked upside the head. So I recommend a guerrilla strike. You sneak up, dart your tongue in there really quick, then dash away before they fully clock what just happened.

And you need to know that they're probably gonna be mad at you. If humans get their own ears wet from a shower or swimming, they're fine with it. But wet ears from tongues, for some reason, get them fired up. It's really funny, actually, so long as you don't let them catch you. Just stay out of their reach until they run out of breath and swear they'll get you later.

But don't worry about that, because they don't *stay* mad. The important thing is that they stay in the present, and if slipping them a little ear-tongue accomplishes that, it's worth the risk.

We can learn from the past, but we can never do anything about it. We can't do anything about the future either. All we can do is live in the present and make good choices about *that* time—because, in a very real sense, it is the only time that actually exists. It's this moment.

And right then I felt a surge of love for Atticus. I mean, I always love him, but sometimes it swells and I feel gooey, like a marshmallow in a microwave. And it's because that bathtime story was like a really good bone. It got better the more I chewed on it.

Story times are great times. The Ten Booms were great humans who knew how to spend their time wisely, and I bet they loved story time as well.

I wondered if there were still any watches around that the Ten Booms worked on while they were alive. They'd be pretty awesome pieces, I bet, that kept time well and reminded us how best to spend it.

My tail thumped drowsily against my bed as I drifted off into a cozy nap. I'd eat something delicious when I woke up. That would be a pretty dang good time too. Boomshakalaka!

*no cats were harmed by any ceilings during that one time when nothing happened

THE GROCERY SACK OF ROME

Did you know there are poisonous lizards in Arizona called Gila monsters? They're black and orange–which to my eyes looks like black and slightly less black–and when they're curled up they resemble burned cinnamon rolls until they move and bite you. Ask me how I know.

Okay, you don't have to ask me: One of them bit me. It looked like some angry poop but it smelled like chicken! So it wasn't my fault. What kind of hound would I be if I didn't investigate chicken smells? We have standards, you know.

Standard Hound Protocol states that when you think something might smell like chicken, you have to investigate in case it actually is chicken and you can eat it. And because I had once had something called Cajun Blackened Chicken, I was kind of hopeful that this black mass on the rocks was a discarded chicken loaf or something. Stranger things have happened to food! Humans throw away perfectly good stuff all the time! So I was completely justified in confirming whether the

Possible Chicken was Actual Chicken, and did not deserve to be attacked by a monster! BECAUSE IT WAS A MONSTER.

Humans did not name them Mildly Ornery Lizards for a very good reason. And the reason is that Gila monsters are legitimately monstrous.

One thing that makes Gila monsters a different kind of reptile from snakes is that when they bite, they don't let go. They lock their jaws on you and kinda gnaw on your flesh and that process injects poison, which means you can't effectively run away and get help because you're dragging around an angry poisonous poop monster that wants to kill you. Which is what I was doing as I barked and yelped in pain and also mentally shouted, <Atticus, help! The poop is trying to kill me! It hurts!>

The Gila monster was attached to my front leg on the right side and I couldn't shake it off. I was basically running with three legs and my Boston terrier buddy, Starbuck, came over to bark at the monster and would have attacked if I didn't warn him off.

<No, don't bite it, Starbuck, it will hurt me more if you tug on it!> I said. <Ow! It hurts! Atticuuuuus!>

Oberon, what is it? His voice in my head calmed me down like, one iota. An iota sounds like it should be an electric car but it just means a super tiny amount, as in *I don't want a single iota of mustard on my sausage*, and I had learned this word recently when Rose–the nice human Atticus loves now–asked if I didn't have an iota of sympathy for squirrels. (The answer, of course, was no.) We were some distance away from him but not out of mental shouting range. He was still over by the patch of land by Tony Cabin in the Superstition Mountains that he'd been trying to heal up for years now. He was close to finishing his work and he really wanted to get that off his to-do list, which was why we were there instead of Tasmania.

<Something is trying to kill me! It's eating my leg!>

I'm on my way. Keep making noise.

<No problem,> I said, and I let the yipes flow the way spice did on Dune because it really hurt. Gila monster venom, I found out later, is the most painful stuff there is.

<What is this thing?> Starbuck asked, barking at the creature as he kept pace with me. <Is it a mutant squirrel? Bad squirrel!>

<I don't know but I don't like it! This is worse than cats!>

<The musical?>

<I meant regular cats, but yeah, that too.>

It was only ten more years or so of running before Atticus got there, though I probably didn't count time correctly because I never do, and I was feeling pain in my whole body, not just my leg. Atticus said I had disturbed a Gila monster, and that's where I learned its name and that it was poisonous and if we had killed it, he would have a much more difficult time getting it off me, because its jaws would have locked on my leg and never let go.

But Atticus was able to get inside its head and convince it to let me go, and after it scurried away, he got to work on breaking down the poison in my blood and healing me up.

Atticus sighed in frustration. "This is a mess," he said. "I'm not going to be able to finish my work here today. We need to get you a bath."

<I'm sorry, Atticus. I was just trying to figure out if the Gila monster was food and now I know that it wasn't and I won't make that mistake again.>

"Didn't you know about them before?"

<If I did, I forgot. But I won't forget this.>

"I hope not. Come on, let's go home and get you in the tub."

<Are you too mad to tell me a story?>

"I'm not mad. Just frustrated at the inconvenience. I'll tell you a story about a guy who got into a whole lot of trouble because of food."

<Did he conduct raids in search of sausage?>

"Metaphorically speaking, yes."

<I can tell already he was a noble figure. Was he a king?>

"Yes."

<I knew it! This is going to be a great bathtime.>

When we got home to Tasmania using an Old Way that allowed us to travel the planes, Starbuck went to the backyard to patrol for squirrels while I got into the bathtub, tail already wagging. Atticus got me all wet with the spray hose attachment thingie and then squirted me with soap.

"Okay," he said. "Story time."

Back in the fourth and fifth centuries I moved around the outskirts of the Roman Empire quite a bit, hanging out with various Germanic tribes who hated Rome and therefore were kindred spirits to me. There were several that I spent time with, but the two that made the most difference in bringing down Rome were the Goths and the Visigoths.

The Goths were pushed into Roman territory by the expansion of the Huns; they didn't like Rome at all, but they liked the Huns even less, so they chose the lesser of two evils—or at least, what they thought was the lesser. Rome liked to promise security, but in exchange they demanded such heavy tribute in bodies and crops that there was no true prosperity to be had; the people were sponges to be squeezed to slake the insatiable thirst of the upper classes. That's little different from feudalism or capitalism, and indeed those later systems were basically modeled on the Roman system—but I digress.

Late in the fourth century, a Goth man named Alaric rose to prominence and became king of what would later become known as the Visigoths—which basically meant western Goths, as opposed to the Ostrogoths, or eastern Goths. Alaric was the first legitimate ruler of the Goths since Fritigern, under whose leadership I'd fought at the Battle of Adrianople. Alaric grew up surrounded by men who'd fought in that battle with me—men who knew what incredible assholes the Romans could be, and who also knew the Romans could be beaten. But at the same time, he grew up schooled in the harsh economic realities of the era: You either grew your food and managed somehow to hold on to it, or you took it from someone else. The Romans tried to have it both ways: take over a region and its food production—killing, enslaving, or absorbing the troublemakers into your own army—then protect it from outsiders. It was a pattern of expansion that empires have emulated ever since. So the Goths, caught between the Romans and the Huns, had to make a choice: Attempt to grow their food and protect it from two ravenous empires, or join one empire and hope it was strong enough to protect them from the other. They chose the Romans.

And then they quickly discovered that the tribute the Romans demanded was far too high. They saw little choice but to rebel—but that placed them in the same perilous situation of having to produce their own food and protect it with minimal resources. That is unless they took food from others—or joined the

Roman army and thereby gain access to the food that Rome had already taken from someone else. For years, Alaric did both. He and his band of Visigoths either raided Roman towns to get the supplies they needed, or happily fought for the Romans, so long as they were paid and fed. I joined his band whenever he was raiding the Romans.

I kind of admired his moxie, because he was running the same sort of protection racket that the Romans were running on the villages of their Empire. "Nice place you got here. Would be a shame if someone pillaged it. Pay me, and I'll make sure nothing bad happens." The problem that Alaric faced–wanting his people to govern themselves out of the shadow of the Roman empire–was that governing yourself took resources. You needed significant start-up capital, and of course a place to establish yourself. The Goths had already been displaced by others, and if they wanted to settle down, they'd need to displace someone else in turn. The Romans–and of course many others–had demonstrated that it was easiest to be expansionist and take the wealth of others, either through tribute or taxes or outright slavery, and that was a system copied by colonial powers for centuries afterward. In fact–if you'll let me fast forward through history–the Visigoths eventually settled in what is now France and Spain, were mostly wiped out in France by the Franks, and in Spain they became known as the Hispani, and they went on to become one of those colonial powers that inflicted untold suffering around the world a thousand or so years later.

I wonder sometimes what would have happened in the New World if Alaric and the Visigoths had been wiped out by Stilicho, instead of allowed to go free. Because Stilicho, a Roman general of the Western empire, had defeated Alaric twice and let him go. Stilicho had beef with the Eastern empire and wanted Alaric's Goths, the largest band of barbarians around, to remain a threat. But letting him go really pissed off Honorius, the western Emperor at the time, and after that Alaric had tremendous trouble getting anything out of the Romans.

But he kept trying. He tried so hard to negotiate with them. In the year 408, he laid siege to Rome and got a vast sum of wealth from them in return for lifting the siege, but that wealth didn't give Alaric or the Goths a place to grow and prosper in the long term. That's what he truly wanted, not silks and silver.

The capital of the empire had been moved to Ravenna because Rome had obviously proven vulnerable, so Alaric and his band drifted that way, threatening the capital, and he began negotiations with Honorius, hoping for a longer-term solution. He had some leverage now because of that successful siege, and while negotiations were tough, they were progressing. He was on the verge of attaining a sustainable peace both for Rome and for his people.

I didn't want that. My desire was to see Rome fall because of its role in wiping out Druidry, and if they made peace with Alaric, it could be decades before another force became strong enough to threaten them. So I left Alaric's camp and went to visit another Goth, Sarus, who was in the region and just so happened to hate Alaric's guts. I convinced him to attack Alaric's people, and Alaric interpreted it as betrayal by Honorius, a deliberate provocation in the midst of negotiations, because Sarus had worked for the Romans as a mercenary. Plus, some other developments I don't need to go into here made Honorius overconfident and he declared Alaric an eternal enemy of Rome, with whom he would never negotiate. Fed up with Honorius and simply done with him, Alaric moved his army back to Rome in August of 410. I was with him for that.

Histories say that the Salarian Gate to the north of Rome was opened by slaves–entirely plausible, because of course the slaves would welcome anyone who came to dole out some death and destruction to their enslavers. But it was me. My tattoos marked me as a pagan barbarian, so whoever observed me in action assumed I must have been a slave brought from Gaul or elsewhere to work in the city.

I'd been careful not to use much magic because of course Aenghus Óg was searching for me, but on this occasion, I made an exception. I shifted my form to an owl, flew over the walls with my sword and clothes, and then subdued the guards. With some judicious binding, I opened the gates for the Visigoths to do their thing. They sacked Rome for three days, stealing pretty much everything that wasn't bolted down.

And they also committed plenty of atrocities–I don't wish to sugarcoat that. But at the time, my hope was that Rome's fall would mean humanity might try something else instead of this rapacious consumption and expansion. It was not the first time that my hopes were dashed against the rocks of reality. But at least I got a little bit of revenge for the Druids.

Alaric moved south from Rome, basically chewing up everything in the southern portion of Italy, but he found no lasting peace for his people. The Visigoths eventually left Italy altogether and settled in France and Spain, as I mentioned earlier, inspired by Alaric's ambitions of finding a place outside of Rome to dwell. Alaric, however, didn't go with them; he died from disease less than a year after the fall of Rome, having won and lost many battles and plundered enormous wealth, yet never achieving security or a home for his people. The Roman empire limped along for another sixty-six years after Rome was sacked—my involvement in making sure it ended is a story for another day.

But I think of Alaric often when I see people struggling today. He was called a barbarian merely because he wasn't Roman, yet he was a clever man who wanted prosperity and safety for his people and discovered, time and again, that "civilization" wouldn't let him have it. The system—the bureaucracy and everything—was set up so that he couldn't win. So he did his best to trash the system, and his moderate success there eventually allowed the Visigoths to prosper—they negotiated their land grant in France and Spain after his death. But Alaric was a domino I pushed in a certain direction, and I wonder what would have happened if I had pushed him differently or hadn't pushed at all. He was simply trying to secure a reliable source of groceries, a life goal many people can appreciate.

<I can certainly appreciate it,> I said, as Atticus finished his tale and started rinsing me off. My front leg hardly hurt at all anymore, though it was still a bit tender. <Have I thanked you recently for being a reliable source of groceries?>

"Not in those exact words," Atticus replied, "but I'm aware of your gratitude."

<It sounds like I would have made an excellent king of the Visigoths.>

"Maybe. The greater likelihood is that you would have struggled to eat well on a regular basis, like most people in that time. The wealthy families of Rome—the Senators, mostly—had little to fear regarding their food security. Everyone else was into subsistence agriculture or joined the military since they got fed regularly, mostly by stealing food from others."

<Why is it so easy for us to get groceries now?>

"It's easy for us because I have money. It's not easy for everyone. The various systems of government and economics in the world are still designed to benefit the wealthy first, and therefore everyone wants to be wealthy. If government was focused instead on basic needs for everyone–food, housing, health care–it would be a very different planet."

<Do you want it to be a very different planet?>

"Yes."

<It will be very soon.>

"How so?"

<The prophecy is almost upon us, Atticus.>

"What prophecy?"

<The one about the Triple Nonfat Double Bacon Five-Cheese Mocha!>

"Oh, that one! I forgot. You never gave me the details on that. Who made this prophecy?"

<I can't tell you, Atticus. I signed an incredibly punitive Non-Disclosure Agreement.>

"You did not! You can't sign anything!"

<I gave my solemn word that if I told anyone about it, I'd be a Chihuahua. So I can't tell you. I don't want to be a Chihuahua, Atticus. Think of the anguish and despair of that guy in *Avatar: The Last Airbender* who looks up to the sky and wails, "My cabbages!" That would be my anguish level if I had to be a Chihuahua.>

"Are you speaking literally? You gave your word regarding this prophecy to someone who could turn you into a Chihuahua?"

<If I answer that, I might turn into a Chihuahua.>

"Okay, this is getting weird. Do I need to worry?"

<No, I think it's going to be a better world, Atticus. I mean, the part where it says Double Bacon is a really big hint. You need to dry me off now so I can go have my zoomies with Starbuck and we can plot the sack of Hobart in honor of Alaric the Visigoth.>

"Why do you want to sack Hobart?"

<For groceries, Atticus! I will be Oberon, the Goth Wolfhound of Tasmania! We will steal sausages for three days!>

"I look forward to hearing the details of your plan." He gave me a quick towel-dry and I gave him a quick summary.

<Here's what I have so far: We go there, and then: We steal sausages.>

"Hmm. You might want to workshop that one a little bit."

<Well, yeah. That's why I need the zoomies. Open the door!>

Atticus opened the door and I took off, bursting into the backyard and telling Starbuck we needed to plan a massive sausage heist to secure our place in the history of empires.

<Yes, food!> he said. That's what makes the world go round, after all.

ANOTHER MOUNTAIN TO CLIMB

I promise I didn't do anything to mess up Atticus's Druid stuff this time. We were back by Tony Cabin in Arizona while he finished fixing up that dead area created by Aenghus Óg. I don't remember all the details of that except that this Aenghus guy opened up a portal to hell and then oopsie, fell in. It's generally regarded as a place you don't want to fall into; I'm pretty sure it has like a zero rating on TripAdvisor and some astonishingly bad reviews on Yelp.

Since I'd ruined Atticus's previous attempt to finish his work there by disturbing a poisonous lizard, I did not go anywhere near anything that smelled like chicken this time in case it turned out to be a Gila monster. Instead, Starbuck and I found something called a horny toad.

They were not toads at all, it turned out, but rather lizards with the round body of a toad, and they had horns on their heads and kind of around the sides, so if something tried to eat them sideways they'd get poked in the mouth. They also had very short tails, which made them look even more toad-like. A fun fact I learned about them is they can squirt blood from their eyes as a kind of defensive maneuver specifically against canines and felines! By which I mean coyotes and bobcats, because those animals will often try to eat horny toads. Apparently the taste of their blood is super nasty because they eat a lot of ants.

Starbuck and I didn't try to eat the one we found. I'd learned my lesson about desert animals and didn't think of them as potential snacks anymore. Besides, we didn't need to eat any stabbity, gross lizards when we normally got plenty of delicious food from Atticus. Horny toads were like second-degree anti-sausage. (First degree anti-sausage, of course, would be cauliflower and plants in the onion family that aren't good for dogs.)

We almost didn't see him but he moved just a tiny bit underneath a cholla cactus as we were passing, and that caught our eye.

<Whoa, Starbuck, I think that's an animal there!>

<Food?> my little buddy asked.

<Maybe. It's camouflaged and hard to see, which probably means lots of things like to eat it. But we should stay away in case it's a monster.>

<Good point.>

I called on Atticus through our mental link and described the creature to him, and that's when he said we'd found a horny toad.

There are a decent number of species in North America, but since we're in Arizona, you most likely found a regal horned lizard, he said. *It's best to leave it alone. But spotting one is quite an accomplishment, so congratulations.*

<Is spotting a horny toad a snackworthy event?>

Okay, you each get one snack that counts against your snack penalty.

Both Starbuck and I were currently suffering through a snackless void for different but related reasons. Starbuck had found some discarded food in Tasmania that he said was "spicy" and Atticus told him not to eat it but he ate it anyway. Later it made him sick and he splattered some watery poop on the carpet, and that made both Atticus and Rose upset. Since he wouldn't have been sick if he left the spicy food alone like he was told, Atticus gave him a snack penalty. I came to the defense of my friend and said, "The spice must flow, Atticus!" and that earned me a snack penalty for connecting *Dune* to diarrhea.

We watched the horny toad for a little while longer to see if he moved again but he stayed very still, and that was boring, so we kept exploring the area to see what else we could find. We found a creek to play in and get ourselves all muddy, but it also felt good to cool down a little bit since it was pretty warm outside. Before we knew it, Atticus was calling us back.

I'm finished, finally. The land is restored. We won't have to come back here again, and I'm glad. That was a tall mountain to climb.

<What mountain? We didn't climb a mountain,> Starbuck said.

<He was speaking metaphorically,> I explained. <He means it was a lot of work to achieve his goal.>

<Our goal is to work off our snack penalty,> Starbuck mused, <so is that like climbing a mountain?>

<Yeah! You got it! Good job, Starbuck!>

He spun around in a circle a couple of times, excited to have grasped a metaphor so quickly. It was the part of human language that gave him the most trouble. <We're climbing that mountain! And at the top there are delicious snacks!>

<Exactly!>

<We are mountain climbers! Snack seekers! Can't stop until we reach the top!>

Since we'd gotten muddy and needed a bath when we got home, I got to hop in the tub and make a special request.

<Atticus, do you know any stories about mountain climbers?>

"I do, actually. I got to meet a famous one. Would you like to hear about her?"

<Yes, please.>

Atticus hosed me down and squirted some shampoo into his hand, applying it vigorously to my coat. "Okay, here we go."

Junko Tabei was a Japanese woman who discovered how much she loved mountain climbing when she was a teenager. She climbed to the top of Mount Fuji and beheld stunning vistas, the naked beauty of the world laid out before her, and was overcome by it. The perspective she gained from the climb was all worth it. She wanted to climb as much as possible after that and preserve the natural world, which meant she also became an ardent environmentalist.

In 1975, she became the first woman to achieve the summit of Mount Everest in the Himalayas. She was celebrated worldwide, but especially in Japan, where she became quite famous. Reaching the summit of Mount Everest is not something everyone can do; of the sixteen people who went with her, only she made it to the top, because some got altitude sickness or simply couldn't go on for many other reasons. People die up there from cold or avalanches or lack of oxygen, and myriad other causes that stem from the extreme conditions. Worse, their bodies just stay there. The slopes of Mount Everest today are littered with bodies of people who tried to climb it and died in the process. Plus, there are tons of actual litter from mountaineers.

The garbage that Junko saw on the slopes–plus on many other mountains she climbed–inspired her to organize many "clean-up climbs" throughout her life. But she also organized a women's climbing club in Japan, because mountaineering was dominated by men and many of them, unfortunately, were the patriarchal, misogynistic sort who believed a woman's place was in the kitchen, and some even refused to climb with her. (Junko's own husband, thankfully, was not that sort.) She wrote seven books, and climbed many, many mountains besides Mount Everest.

Her goal was to climb the highest peak in 190 different countries, gaze down from each, and thereby see as much of the planet as she could.

Along the way she climbed the highest peak on each continent, thereby also becoming the first woman to climb the Seven Summits–an extremely rare accomplishment. In addition to Everest for Asia, she climbed Kilimanjaro in Africa, Aconcagua in South America, Denali in North America, Elbrus in Europe, Vinson in Antarctica, and Puncak Jaya in New Guinea, which is counted as part of the continent of Australia, and certainly taller than any mountain in Australia's mainland–it's part of what's known as the Messner List.

I got to meet her in 1991–that was just a few years before you were born and we became friends–when she was climbing Mount Vinson in Antarctica. I was a part of the expedition, and since I spoke fluent Japanese, we talked a bit and I came to admire her as a person who did her best to make her life extraordinary. She saw things most humans never have and never will.

I joined her for a clean-up climb in the Himalayas a couple of years later, and spent some extra time there on my own cleaning what I could without giving away my position to Aenghus Óg.

Unfortunately, she got a cancer diagnosis in 2012, but continued to climb mountains until her death in 2016. She climbed the tallest peaks in sixty countries and saw a whole lot of the planet. She led a truly exceptional life, and I was very sorry to hear of her passing.

She got an asteroid named after her, and there's also a mountain range on Pluto called Tabei Montes, because all geographical features on that planetoid are named after explorers and pioneers. She never did achieve her overall goal, but I know she would have if she could have stayed with us longer. And she had to know she would never make it, near the end. But she never stopped pursuing it, never gave up. I will always honor her as a friend to people, and a friend of Gaia.

<Wow. I'm sorry I didn't get to meet her. She sounds like she would have been a friend to hounds too. You know, we haven't climbed a mountain together in a while! Maybe we should do that soon. Speaking of life goals, Atticus, is there an Old Way that you can use to get us to Seattle?>

"I don't believe so, but I might be able to request that one be made. Why do you ask?"

<Because it's nearly time. We have to go to that secret facility on the outskirts of Seattle.>

"Wait, what?"

<You know. That Research and Development bunker I told you about.>

"I don't remember this."

<It's where they're going to invent the Triple Nonfat Double Bacon Five-Cheese Mocha in accordance with the prophecy.>

"Oh, no. Not this again. You mean the prophecy where you will turn into a Chihuahua if you tell me anything about it?"

<Correct. We need to be at that facility soon.>

"Why?"

<To stop a crime! And to taste that beverage.>

"It doesn't sound like this should be a priority for anyone."

<What? I mean. Come on, wait. I must have screwed up how I presented it to you. Okay. Look at it this way. You want to know who made the prophecy and who is funding this research and who threatened me with turning into a Chihuahua if I told you any details, right? Doesn't that make it a priority?>

"I don't know. When is this happening?"

<In twenty-nine days, four hours, thirteen minutes, and eight seconds.>

"What? Oberon, you are terrible at telling time. How do you know this?"

<I can't tell you. But we gotta be there, Atticus. I'm as serious about this as I am about poodles. Please just trust me on this one thing, okay?>

"Okay." He rinsed me off and closed his eyes as I shook myself, then he unplugged the drain and started toweling me down. "Do you know where this secret research facility is? Should we have the Old Way built soon and maybe conduct a scouting mission?"

<It's in the other direction from wherever Tacoma is. They were trying to avoid the "Tacoma Aroma.">

"Ah, yes, I have experienced that. It's real. I imagine if you were trying to craft something that smelled and tasted good, you wouldn't want your nose messed up by Tacoma. So somewhere north of Seattle. I imagine we'll have travel time no matter what, unless you're able to be more specific than that."

<I can't be because I forgot. Honestly, I didn't think I would ever live long enough to see it. When I heard about the prophecy, I was still in my first normal lifespan and I thought surely something would get me before I had to worry about it, like old age or a great big bear. Something like ninety percent of wolfhounds get got by great big bears, you know.>

"Whoever told you that was spectacularly wrong."

<Well, it sounded right to me. Time for zoomies!>

"No, wait. If you don't know where this facility is, how are we going to find it?"

<I know I'll be able to find it the same way I know what time we have to be there. If you can just get us nearby, I can blaze the trail. Except I won't do that literally. Setting stuff on fire is a bad idea–unless you do it in a controlled situation where you're cooking me something to eat. Then it's a great idea.>

Atticus let me out for zoomies after that, and I told Starbuck he was going to get a great story about a mountain climber when it was his turn. Once my lil' Boston terrier friend was happily hearing about Junko Tabei in the bathtub and I was stretched out on my doggie bed, I wondered if I should set my sights on climbing metaphorical mountains if not literal ones. Normally hounds just want food and love and naps and a chance to chase things, and I got all of those things because I am a very good boy, yes I am. Was it a weakness or a moral failing or something that I didn't want much more than that? Why wasn't I motivated to achieve some lofty goal for my life?

It began to stress me out. What if I'd been doing it wrong all along, which was a very long time because I'm a very old dog? But that didn't make sense. If I was doing it wrong, then wouldn't I be a bad dog? I'm not a bad dog. So why didn't I have mountains to climb like Junko Tabei?

Then I realized she did what she did for the same reasons I do what I do: We both liked to look around and be happy with what we see or saw and oh no I think I have stumbled into one of those time warps with tenses and I don't know which when I was am doing it anymore. Let's just pretend that sentence didn't happen and try again.

Being happy with what you see before you is the mountain we all have to climb. Sometimes, of course, that's impossible. If you are looking at a squirrel, for example, or watching a cable news show, you're not going to be happy. But unless you have something awful like that to deal with, you have the ability to take in your surroundings and wag your tail. Maybe you will have to do a little something to get to your happy place; Junko would climb mountains, and I often have to flop down on top of Atticus's feet to make sure he gets the message that I want a belly rub. The key thing to remember is that happiness is easy to find if you keep it simple.

My stress ran away like a carnivore from carrots as I realized that the way I live my life is actually the mountain a *lot* of people are trying to climb. Their ambition is to live without ambition. I am living the dream. I have achieved the summit of contentment.

I think Junko Tabei and I would have been great friends.

THE HUMAN DYNAMO

I have made it clear on several occasions that English is a ridiculous language that contains many expressions that make no sense. One of the most offensive, however, is *prairie dog*.

Prairie dogs are not any kind of dog! They are more like a chubby squirrel. (Atticus said they aren't like a squirrel chubby either but didn't explain what he meant by that. He seemed to think it was funny though.)

Atticus told Starbuck and me that we could chase all the prairie dogs we wanted and inform them they're not dogs while he worked on shutting down a fracking site in Oklahoma. It had been causing earthquakes and poisoning the groundwater and the local elemental was very unhappy, so Atticus agreed to forcibly decommission it for a while.

Here's the thing about prairie dogs: They live in extensive underground tunnel systems and they talk to each other. I couldn't catch any of them and I couldn't dig down far enough to get them. Starbuck couldn't either. And as soon as we'd focus on one hole, they'd pop up out of another one and chitter at us, and when we ran over there, they disappeared and popped up at yet another location. It was sort of like that carnival game, Whack-a-Mole, except we never successfully whacked a single one.

We were run down in fairly short order. And exhausted, and thoroughly frustrated with prairie dogs, and pretty sure we'd hold a grudge forever, or at least until our next nap. And we were so covered in Oklahoma dust that little clouds of it poofed off us with every step. (I think I remember some documentary mentioning that Oklahoma had a whole bowl of dust at one time, but they never explained why people wanted a dust bowl or why it was historically significant, except that maybe they grew some super angry grapes in it. No, they didn't use the word *angry*. Was it mad? No. Wrath! Yeah, wrath! Though I'm not sure if grapes of wrath would make red or white wine. Idioms don't give me any helpful hints either because you see red when you're angry and you can also have a white-hot rage. Maybe grapes of wrath give you a nice rosé? If I had paid closer attention to the documentary I might remember better, but a poodle walked by outside and that distracted me. I can remember the poodle very well. She had a cinnamon coat and she looked incredibly smart. I bet she could do algebra and maybe even taxes, and I never even got to go outside and sniff her ass. Anyway, she's why I don't know more about Oklahoma. Which is not to saddle her with an ounce of blame. She was perfect. But my knowledge of dust bowls is imperfect due to my own peccadilloes.)

(I should get a snack for using *peccadilloes* in a sentence.)

When Atticus called us back, his industrial sabotage completed and the fracking site defunct for a while, he noticed right away that we were dirty, dirty dogs.

"Gods below, you two, how did you get that filthy?"

<Prairie rodents, Atticus! It's all their fault!>

See there, pups? Poodles: Blameless. Prairie dogs? Blame them for *everything*.

Starbuck added, <We just wanted to yell at them because they shouldn't pretend to be dogs, but they wouldn't stay still and listen!>

"Yes, it's shocking that the tiny rodents didn't stay still for the predator with large teeth. But I'm unimpressed with your excuse. The prairie dogs do not call themselves dogs and are unaware that humans do. You're blaming them for nothing and not taking responsibility for your own actions."

<Okay. I like to chase things and don't care about getting dirty because I am Oberon, Proud Protector of the Plains!>

Starbuck chimed in. <I am Starbuck, Who Needs a Fancy Title! I never have one ready. Uhh...I need to think about this.>

We tried to convince Atticus to let us nap before we got a bath because we were so tired from executing our Prairie Dog Correction Protocols, but he wouldn't hear it.

"You can sleep when you're clean," he said.

<But we can also sleep when we're dirty,> I said.

"How about this? Take a bath or take a snack penalty."

Starbuck barked. <No penalty! Soap me and snack me!>

<Can't we get an Exhaustion Waiver just this once?>

"Nope. If you get Rose's house all dirty, I'm going to be the one who pays for it."

That's how I wound up getting a bath earlier than I wanted. But at least there would be a story, and I told Atticus that it should be invigorating.

"For energy, eh? Okay. I can tell you about a guy who electrified the world."

Lots of what I do as a Druid now is frantically try to heal up gaping wounds in the earth caused by industrial activities. And many of these activities had their origins in the nineteenth century, as a host of inventions and scientific discoveries allowed humans to extract and exploit natural resources faster than ever before. I don't wish to imply that the discoveries were universally negative. Many of them were great. But one man in particular experimented in a wide range of areas, and his discoveries—and popularization of them—are responsible for a large part of what is wondrous and horrific in modern society.

His name was Michael Faraday, and he lived in London. His early work in chemistry isolated benzene, a toxic chemical that found its way into many petroleum products and plastics polluting the planet today. But he also did a lot of very important work in electricity and magnetism, leading to much of the world's modern conveniences. Think of how much of the world runs on electricity now. It's a fundamental part of our infrastructure. But before Michael Faraday, light came from candles or oil lanterns. His work allowed humans to transition to electric power and therefore spawned all these electronic devices that we find so indispensable today.

I got to meet him in 1839. He'd been engaged in nonstop experimentation for ten years, working frenetically and driving himself to a nervous breakdown. Which can mean many things, but basically he'd worked himself to a mental and physical shutdown–much like you and Starbuck when you chase prairie dogs too long. He was burned out.

I found him on a park bench, hair parted down the middle, posture impeccable, tossing crusts of bread to pigeons and looking fairly engaged by the activity. Not in a birdwatching sense; it was more that he was looking for patterns in their movement, almost as if he were practicing augury, and that drew my attention when I otherwise would have passed him by. I was in London on some unrelated business but it wasn't pressing, so I took my ease and bid him good day. He grunted at me.

"I do hope I'm not intruding," I said, in my best posh English accent.

"No, no, carry on," he said.

"My thanks. What business do the pigeons augur today?"

"Augur?" he said. "I'm no pagan mystic. I'm a devout Christian."

"Oh. I beg your pardon. I didn't mean to suggest otherwise. I was merely making conversation. There does seem to be a method to their movement, even if it is not for divination."

"That's true enough."

"They are mysteries to be solved. So much of the world is, yet we are making progress every day."

"Well. Perhaps not every day. Scientists need some time off now and again."

"You sound like you're speaking from experience."

"A bit, yes."

Taking a risk, I decided to lay my fictional identity and backstory on him in the hope that he would share his. "Cornelius Fotheringham at your service."

<Atticus, whoa, wait. I didn't even know that was possible! You fathered a ham?>

"What? No. It was just an incredibly English surname I was using at the time."

<But you taught me that English surnames are based on things people did. The Smiths were blacksmiths, the Millers were millers, the Taylors were tailors. So that means at some point in that family's history, somebody fathered a ham.>

"No, Oberon, it wasn't like that—"

<Don't hold back on me, Druid! This is the most interesting human family name of all time!>

"Okay, I can see you're fixated on this. So let's suppose that the Fotheringhams were hog farmers, and metaphorically, if not biologically, they could have fathered a ham in the butchering process."

<Well, why didn't they just call themselves the Butcher family, then?>

Atticus shrugged. "Maybe they liked hams."

<Oh. I guess it's hard to argue with that.>

"Let's get back to it, shall we? I told the man I was at his service and involved in botany."

"Fascinating chemicals in plant life," he said. "I'm something of a chemist myself. Michael Faraday."

And that is when I realized to whom I was speaking: One of the leading minds of the age. He'd published the laws of electrolysis a few years earlier, a process that's foundational to industrial chemistry today, wherein he popularized terms such as electrode and ion. He'd made the first electric generator eight years before, which of course became the basis of all future technology that used electricity. And he'd invented what's known now as the Faraday Cage, which shields whatever's inside from electromagnetic forces or signals from the outside. I'd caught one of his early Christmas lectures at the Royal Institution and said so, then apologized for not recognizing him.

"Oh, not to worry. I'm sure I don't look as well as the day you saw me."

"Are you feeling poorly?"

"No. Well, yes, but not from any disease. Unless it is of the mind. I have suffered a nervous episode of some kind and don't feel like working. Which makes me feel like a failure—I must be, for here I am prattling on to a stranger. Forgive me."

"Nonsense. All of it. I mean, not the nervous episode. That's real. But it doesn't make you a failure. If I have learned anything as a botanist that can apply to my life, it's recognizing that all things have their season. Spring has come and gone: It was good for a time, then it ended. But that does not mean spring was a failure. It was bloody fantastic while it lasted. All things end and are replaced by some new beginning. So you had a period of work and now you are in a period of rest. You will work again—and it might be some completely new field that nourishes your soul—and that too will be good so long as it lasts. I have not always been a botanist, nor will I continue to be one much longer. New seasons of my life are coming. And I feel certain there will be another productive season ahead for you when it's time. At no point have you been a failure, Mr. Faraday."

He said nothing at first, and I apologized for lecturing a lecturer.

"No, no, Mr. Fotheringham, your views are welcome. So it is your position that my sitting here, doing nothing productive beyond feeding the pigeons, is in fact productive if I view it as a period of rest rather than idleness?"

"Correct. Think of it as a field lying fallow for a season. Without rest, the field bears poor crops. Give it a chance to replenish itself, and it becomes bountiful once more. Combine that with rotation—planting different crops that require different nutrients—and you have a sustainable plan for growth that will last a lifetime."

Faraday nodded once. "That's very comforting. A kind and generous analogy."

"And accurate. Seasons are woven into our existence. Cycles perpetuate as do night and day. It is fruitless to dwell on the past, for there is the current season to enjoy and the future to look forward to."

That earned me a side-eye. "Begging your pardon, Mr. Fotheringham, but what is your age? I can't imagine you have much of a past."

I grinned at him. "I'm much older than I look. But I am hopeful for many more seasons of good work ahead, in whatever field that next takes my fancy."

"I'm glad you decided to take your ease. It's been entirely pleasant."

"It has been a very great privilege, and I look forward to your next Christmas lecture, whensoever it occurs."

I took my leave but checked in every so often with Mr. Faraday's work. He did indeed get back to it soon enough. He made special glass for use in lighthouses. He devised methods of protecting ship hulls from corrosion. He determined that explosions in coal mines were facilitated by coal dust, thereby leading to better ventilation in all mines and fewer explosions. And he discovered diamagnetism, the idea that some materials are repulsed by magnetic fields. And I caught another of his lectures some years later: *First Principles of Electricity* in 1843.

Very few people have had greater impact on our modern lives than Mr. Faraday. He invented what became a dynamo, and was himself something of a human dynamo, bringing tremendous energy to his work, which in turn energized the world. He was a rare genius–like Galileo or Van Gogh. I feel lucky to have met him, however briefly.

<Do hounds have seasons, Atticus?>

"Of course."

<Well, what are my seasons? I mean, ever since I can remember it's been sausage season, and I hope that never ends. And poodle season! Great big bears, Atticus, poodle season should last for billions and billions of years!>

"You were a puppy for a season, and then you were a full-grown adult."

<That's it? Just two seasons?>

"No. I think you've had plenty of seasons as an adult. For a while you insisted that you were Snugglepumpkin. Then you were Oberon Snackworthy. Almost every time I give you a bath, in fact, you enjoy a new season."

<Oh! That's right! That means it's time for another one. I am Oberon, the Canine Dynamo! Let me out of this bath and I'll prove it to you with a legendary case of the zoomies!>

"You have the energy for that? I thought you were exhausted from Prairie Dog Correction Protocols."

<I have been revivified by bubbles.>

"You have? Oh, you're going to want a snack for using *revivified* in a sentence."

<You are correct.>

He gave me a quick towel dry and a snack before I zoomed outside with gusto, though Starbuck was lying down and for once didn't join me. He was snoozing and I made only one circuit of the yard before I slowed down and thought about how nice my bed would feel.

<I'm still a dynamo,> I said, even though Starbuck had no idea what I was talking about and my tone was anything but dynamic. <I just don't think it's zooming season right now. I need some time to recharge. On the other side of a nap and maybe a steak, I'll have some serious zooming to do. The Canine Dynamo will spark joy, mark my words!>

<I don't know all those words,> Starbuck said.

As I curled up on my bed inside, I thought about how many seasons Atticus has had. More than nearly everyone, I think. So many places he's lived and jobs he's done, so many relationships and cuisines from around the world. I think he's had, like, *all* the sausages. I should ask him how he knows when it's time to end one season and start another.

But I think I'm a pretty decent Canine Dynamo, because I was doing things the way Faraday did: An overarching goal made up of much smaller goals. He wanted to discover how the world worked, so he applied science to it in many different fields. I want to eat all the meats, so I'm applying teeth to it in many different countries—also fields, I guess, except actual fields instead of fields of study.

After I take a proper nap, I'm going to seek out something new. I wonder what hippos taste like? Does anyone even know? Aren't they just giant tanks that kill a hundred times more people than sharks every year? Why isn't everyone terrified of hippos, which are bigger than great big bears? Why don't we have a movie about them being involved in an extreme weather event? Like HIPPONADO.

I would totally watch a whole season of that.

THE TRIPLE NONFAT DOUBLE BACON FIVE-CHEESE MOCHA

A long time ago, I was paid a visit by someone I cannot name under pain of being turned into a Chihuahua. That is a particularly heinous pain to be under, because I am an extraordinarily handsome Irish wolfhound and the thought of becoming a Chihuahua has given me nightmares. In one of them, a rich lady wearing too much perfume scooped me up and put me in her purse and took me to brunch where she fed me a few crumbs of buttered English muffin. The indignity of being placed in a purse, unable to hunt or sniff any asses! And how humiliating to be fed carbs instead of protein! The harrowing lack of sausage—not even a highly processed Vienna sausage!—has made me feel sorry for Chihuahuas ever since. What a terrible fate it would be to live as a brunch dog! I woke up whimpering and so distraught that I had to be comforted with bratwurst.

This person I cannot name spake unto me a prophecy. (I suppose I could have said they *told* me a prophecy, but when you throw around words like *prophecy* you might as well say things like "verily, in sooth, he spake unto me" because they really pair well with *prophecy*, whereas they don't work so well with *a joke*. Try it: "Verily, he spake unto me a joke." See? It doesn't work. I am trying to become a word connoisseur and appreciate pairings because when I share these observations with Atticus he gives me more snacks.)

The prophecy regarded a scientist in a white lab coat who would emerge at an appointed time from a secret underground lab holding an impossible drink: The Triple Nonfat Double Bacon Five-Cheese Mocha. It was impressed upon me that we (meaning Atticus and I, because Starbuck was not in the picture at the time) had to be there when the scientist emerged so that we could prevent a serious crime. The nature of the crime was not shared with me. I deduced that the drink itself was not the crime because he was going to appear with it first and then we must prevent whatever villainy might occur. My secret hope was that he might spill a little bit of the drink and the part with the bacon in it would land where I could lap it up. The digestive system of dogs wasn't friendly with chocolate so I wasn't interested in the mocha part, just the bacon part.

The secret lab, however, was evidently not so secret, since the person who spake unto me the prophecy knew of its location years in advance. I was told that I'd be able to find it because it would give off a certain *effluvium*, which is a snack-earning word I encourage everyone to use, and I would be able to smell that effluvium, distinguish it from the vast panoply of other human effluvia, and navigate to the precise spot we needed to be. I reminded Atticus of the date and time on a few occasions, and he decided we should leave a full day beforehand to ensure we could find the right place before the appointed hour.

"It would be good to arrive early, scout approaches and vulnerabilities, and find a place to wait," he said, and then he got loaded for bear.

I liked that expression, for there are few things so dangerous as a great big bear, and if you are loaded for one it gives you confidence that you can emerge from any confrontation alive and possibly triumphant. Curiously, according to Atticus, getting loaded for bear did not mean including any bear spray. It did mean that he filled up a rucksack with things he normally didn't, like a box of illegal throwing stars dipped in a paralytic poison, a small tent since he anticipated rain, and one of these fancy camp stove setups where he'd be able to make a pour-over coffee and fry up some sausages for us that he was packing in an insulated container. And he brought his magic hatchet, of course, which he'd been fond of for quite some time now.

He didn't have Fragarach anymore, but that hatchet had sigils drawn on it and I think he told me Criedhne was making him a new enchanted one, a named weapon like Fragarach or Granuaile's Scáthmhaide. It would have permanent enchantments on it to make it super mega dangerous, whereas the one with sigils was merely dangerous in the extreme, because the sigils wore off after a while and he had to re-ink them.

A few weeks ago, he'd asked Coriander to request that an Old Way be built in Seattle so we could go there and begin our journey north. Bizarrely, he didn't have it made in any sort of natural spot: He had it built right underneath Pike Place Market in Ghost Alley, a tunnel underneath the market crafted with old stone and brick and covered over with chewing gum and antifascist political posters. When we arrived there and he put Starbuck and me on a leash while we were in city limits, I asked him why he chose it.

"Ghost Alley Espresso," he explained. They had turmeric and shroom lattes and other drinks humans like made with hot bean juice and cow squirts. I guess he really wanted those, because he bought two for himself and then got Starbuck and me little cups full of whipped cream.

He flagged down a taxi after that and we drove to a park in one of the northern suburbs, where he was hoping I'd be able to find that effluvium and give us a general direction to go. He was also going to top up the energy in his bear charm so that he could feed it to us as needed while we ran in the paved portions of human settlements with no connection to the earth.

<Which way, Oberon?> Starbuck asked, and I took big snuffles of the air in every direction before I focused in on something weird. Most of what I smelled—car exhaust, urine, city smells like that—could be found most anywhere. There were some ocean smells and three kinds of cat shit too. But there was a coppery, bitter tang to the air that you didn't smell anywhere else—definitely some kind of effluvium—and it was north and a bit east of us.

<Sniff this way,> I told him. <Smell that weird thing? It's like blood but not exactly. Metallic and rich like red velvet cake.>

<Cake! Yes food!>
<Do you smell it?>
<Yes! I smell it!>
<I think that's where we're going.>

And so the long run began. Since it was going to be a thing that took some time and we had nothing else to do, Atticus told us about the first marathon run by Pheidippides, which probably did not actually happen, but the fictional account of it inspired many nonfictional marathons, so that was an extremely rare instance of misinformation turning out to be all right in the end, as opposed to misinformation online that led to people making terrible life decisions that drained their life savings or even killed them.

Apparently this fictional first marathon was quite different from modern marathons, because there were no water stations along the route to keep the runner hydrated, no one cheering and clapping and saying, "Come on, Pheidippides, you got this, bud!" So what he supposedly did was run all the way to Athens, inform them that some invading Persians had been defeated, and then he promptly died on the spot, presumably staining the marble as his sphincters relaxed. This is why we have hydration stations along marathon routes today: Nobody likes dead guys shitting on their floor. But our marathon to the source of the effluvium was full of rest stops and interesting smells and at one point, a spirited scolding of a squirrel.

When we finally reached our destination, I knew it like someone had set off a tuning fork in my bones. We were in Snohomish County by the Snohomish River just south of the city of Snohomish. (You may have snohomishly noticed that I like to say Snohomish.) We stood on a property that Atticus said was used primarily for weddings because it was so scenic and full of birdsong. There were rustic buildings at one end and small stands of timber and undergrowth to serve as windbreaks across an expanse of otherwise uninterrupted meadow. Steaks on the hoof lowed and chewed their grass in a distant pasture. The land undulated in soft waves in every direction, broken only by the river to the west of us. And at the top of one of those waves there was a small exhaust port nearly hidden in the grasses. It was the sort of target you'd probably miss unless you used to bullseye womp rats back on Tatooine.

<This is it, Atticus. That's the source of the effluvium. Whatever's going to happen is going to happen here.>

We all sort of looked around, bewildered. It didn't seem like there was anything happening at all.

"Well, I guess you weren't kidding about the secret part of the secret lab. Let's see what the elemental can tell me."

His eyes unfocused for a bit and Starbuck decided that was his cue to nip at my heels and play. We chased each other around in that pleasant meadow until Atticus called us back.

"There's quite a compound underneath here. I'm guessing three subterranean levels and none of it connects to the farm buildings, though I'm sure the owners of this land know it's here. You can't construct something like this and have no one notice. Though it probably wouldn't have been noticed by anyone else but the owner. Look around. It's just fields and river. No roads nearby. Buildings we can see are distant and mostly obscured by trees around the houses, which means they would have had a screened view of the construction while it was going on."

<So how do the scientists get in or out? Where are their cars?>

"The entrance is right over here," Atticus said, pointing to the north where the hill dropped or dipped down fairly steeply. It would be fun to roll down that little hill or even sled down it in the winter. "There's a hidden door on this side, according to what the elemental told me. Very well done—can't see any indication that it exists. I wonder how long they seal themselves up in there. They must bring in weeks of supplies at a time."

<This is like the secret lab underneath the laundromat in *Breaking Bad*. Whoa! Atticus, what if they're cooking drugs down there and that's the source of the effluvium? And what if one of the cooks has a coffee side project going like Walter White's assistant guy? That must be what is going on. Otherwise why would anyone go to all that trouble and expense to keep coffee recipes a secret?>

"I don't think anyone would," Atticus replied. "But I don't think it's drugs. The smell—what little of it I can detect with my human nose—isn't what you'd get from drug cooking. And there's no evidence of a distribution system in place here. No tire tracks, I mean. No way to get the theoretical drugs out and supplies in."

<Vehicles in a meadow would draw attention. But horses wouldn't,> I said. <Or they could be using drones. You said those are all the rage nowadays.>

"Those are good points, but I think there is something else going on down there, and tomorrow, presumably, we'll find out. Is that countdown still going on in your head?"

<Yes. The man will emerge tomorrow morning at 8:09 a.m. and we will need to do something, but I don't know what.>

"We should find a spot to camp for the evening," Atticus said, and immediately cast his gaze north. There was a stand of trees and assorted undergrowth there at the riverbend that looked like it would allow us to hide ourselves well—and it would essentially be invisible from the property's buildings because of the rolling terrain.

Atticus wasn't particularly respectful of the concept of trespassing. He figured the whole earth was his to walk around on if he wanted. He'd treat it better than anyone who said they owned it.

The elemental was super happy to have us there. It basically cleared a nice spot for our tent, moved over a boulder for Atticus to sit on, another to serve as a food prep surface, and then grew some extra undergrowth to the south so no one would be able to see us unless they walked right into our camp.

Atticus had gotten pretty good at putting up a tent with only one hand and my help. I'd hold a pole or stake or whatever in place while he did something at another end, and it went pretty fast. Once he had the tent all set, he got out his little camp stove kit and started to fry up some sausages for us: he had apple bacon and some duck sausage that he'd scored from some fancy butcher shop in Launceston, and they were delicious. Since we were very tired from our running and we felt full and snuggly, we fell asleep as soon as it got dark and woke with the dawn to the songs of robins, larks, and warblers. Atticus did his coffee thing and cooked us more sausages, and we had everything packed and ready to go once we finished with whatever situation was coming. He left out his box of throwing stars and hatchet, and then we crept forward to the edge of the copse where we had an unobstructed view of the hillside where there was supposedly an entrance to a subterranean lab.

"Prepare yourselves," he said around seven thirty. "I'm going to cast camouflage." He liked to warn us because it tickled. The binding did something with the pigments in our fur and skin and it can startle a hound if he's not expecting it.

We melted from view, though of course I could hear Starbuck breathing. He is not a stealthy breather. And then we had some time to kill so Atticus started to tell us about Benjamin Franklin and how often the founding father of the United States ran around naked. "That portrait of him on the hundred-dollar bill where he's got that tiny smile? It's because he wasn't wearing any pants," he explained.

I was just about to question him about how he knew that when Starbuck and I heard some movement off to the east.

<Someone coming,> Starbuck said.

There were some dudes moving our way in tactical gear—camouflage prints that weren't nearly as effective as Atticus's camouflage and grease smeared on their faces—and they had guns because we were in America.

Using our mental link, Atticus said, *Stay quiet and still. Let's watch.*

The men—eight of them, I think, which means they might have a name like a squad or a platoon—surrounded the little hill. One of them settled down very close to us, lying prone and facing the hillside where the door was supposed to be. He had a little tripod thing to keep the barrel of his gun steady.

Well, I think I have an idea about what sort of crime we're supposed to prevent, Atticus said. *Very curious about who these guys are and what they're after. I'm sure it's not the mocha.*

<You think maybe it's organized crime?>

I think they're organized and intend to commit a crime, but I don't think this a mob or a cartel. These look like mercenaries. The question is who paid them to be here and what they're supposed to accomplish. Hmm. Guys with guns usually don't feel like talking. They take the attitude that they don't have to talk so long as they have a gun to point at you. Maybe I can do something about that with the elemental's help.

He fell silent after that, no doubt communicating with the elemental, and soon afterward I heard a startled if low-volume oath uttered from the mercenary nearby. His gun and tripod were sinking into the earth. His hands sank for a bit too as he tried to yank the gun back, but eventually he let go and was left there cursing and at least partially disarmed. Muffled swearing rose to the heavens all around because these were the kinds of guys who thought they'd die before they let someone take their guns. You can't argue with the earth, though.

This is fairly amusing, Atticus said as we listened to them demanding answers from each other about what the hell just happened. *But let's see what they do next.*

What they did was rearm themselves with handguns. *Suboptimal,* Atticus judged. *It's eight o'clock now. I don't want eight guys to have the advantage over whoever emerges from the bunker. I only want myself to have the advantage.*

He had the elemental swallow up their legs: The ground underneath their legs sank and then reformed over the top, effectively preventing them from moving anywhere, yet leaving their asses exposed. This was key because they were easy targets and lacked any armor, unlike their torsos, which were covered in bulletproof vests. Like playing a game of duck-duck-goose, I carried the open box of throwing stars in my mouth and Atticus tossed one into each of the butts of the mercenaries, who loudly complained that something unseen had bitten them. By the time he'd made a full circuit and I laid down the box, the paralytic toxin was taking effect on the first guy, and it was simple for Atticus to step on his wrist, strip the gun out of his hand, and toss it away. We continued like that until there was a silent, unarmed ring of mercenaries half-buried in the meadow. And shortly after he disarmed the final one, the hillside groaned and shook and scraped as a hidden door tore through roots and turf and gave me an extra dose of that effluvium mixed in with human body odor and deodorant.

A white man in a super white lab coat emerged, scruffy and squinting, holding a coffee mug in his right hand that had an illustration of a spacefaring capybara on it. He had some dark unkempt hair and thick-rimmed glasses, but once he stood in full sun he turned his face up, took a deep breath, and then exhaled in great pleasure as he smiled.

"Heck yeah, fresh air," he said.

Let's circle around behind him, quietly, Atticus said, and we did as best we could, though he did hear us and turn around just as Atticus dropped the camouflage.

"Jesus!" he said. "Who are you?"

"Not Jesus. I'm a good guy who means you no harm," he said, "as opposed to the eight mercenaries who were lying in wait for you. Any idea who sent them?"

"What mercenaries?"

"They're spread out around your door here. They had guns, but they don't now. They're neutralized for the moment but will be actively trying to achieve their goal again soon. Any ideas about what that might be?"

"They want to destroy us, I imagine."

"Why?"

"Because they're probably on the payroll of a petroleum company. We're a biscuit away from making them obsolete. If they've found us, we need more security."

"I'd say so."

"I shouldn't have come out. I need to get back inside."

"Sure. I'm delighted to hear you're working on some kind of energy solution. The planet could definitely use it. But before you go, I need you to tell me about your drink."

He looked at his mug, then back at us. "This?"

"Yes. That's not a regular coffee, is it?"

"No. But why do you care?"

"Is it a new invention you made yourself?"

"Yeah," he said, his tone guarded.

"So tell me about it. Then you can go back inside, call reinforcements."

"Okaaay. It's...well. It's a Triple Nonfat Double Bacon Five-Cheese Mocha."

"Outstanding. Is it any good?"

"The best I've ever had. When you're trapped underground for weeks at a time you develop hobbies, and weird coffee is my thing now."

"Fascinating. Okay. You obviously start with a triple shot of espresso. Then nonfat milk. But after that I get confused."

"I added back in the fat that got skimmed from the milk. You treat the bacon fat like a syrup: Two pumps, or two tablespoons. Which means a full ounce, basically. So that's the double bacon. Then the five-cheese blend is frothed in, which lends you some more fat but also some smoothness, some silkiness, and a bit of salt to cut bitterness. No actual cheese flavor. Then of course your sweetness comes from the mocha."

"That sounds extraordinary. Unique, perhaps. Would you mind if I had a sip?"

"Oh. Well." He clearly had doubts.

"I hate to be indelicate, but there were eight mercenaries ready to assassinate you. Or breach your facility. Whatever. Give me a sip and we're square."

"Right. Thanks. That seems like a good deal."

He handed over the mug to Atticus and he took a delicate slurp from the rim. Then his eyes lit up. "Gods below, man. You may have made the best mocha in the history of the world."

"Thanks."

He returned the cup without giving Starbuck or me a single lick of it. We came *all that way* and *got nothing*.

We complained mentally to Atticus and the mocha guy must be empathetic to dogs, because he said, "I think your dogs want some."

"Oh, they certainly do. They have a great Resting Beg Face. But I'll take care of them later. All right. In you go. Call your reinforcements. I'll collect all the firearms and pile them up in front of the door, but leave the guys where they are. They'll snap out of their funk soon, so get yourself buttoned up and tell your help to hurry."

"You never told me who you are."

"Neither did you. I'm someone who'd like to be free of fossil fuels and you're someone working on the problem. Today I helped you, and soon you're going to help everyone, right?"

"We hope so, yeah."

"Good. Let's leave it at that."

"But...why are you here? And how did you take out eight mercenaries by yourself?"

"I had help. But as to why I'm here, it's because I was told to be, but I don't know who sent me."

"Well, it's that kind of facility, I guess. Secrets upon secrets."

"Will you share the secret of your five-cheese blend, and how much you used?"

"I'll give you a hint: They are all Spanish cheeses."

"Fair enough. Thank you, sir. Be safe." Atticus moved out of the way of the door and the nameless scientist nodded his thanks.

"You too."

He disappeared into the vault and it slid shut, presenting an unbroken grassy hillside again, and I had questions.

<Why didn't you ask him for a tour? Or ask what they're making? Or at least get him to make us our own mocha?>

"It's not a tourist facility, and it doesn't really matter what they're making. We weren't sent to learn that."

<How do you know? I never told you why we had to be here.>

"You said we had to prevent a crime and we did. Was there something else?"

<Yes. But I'm still not sure if I can tell you.>

"Keep an eye on the mercenaries while I pile up the guns, please? One of you take this side, one of you take the other side of the hill. And I promise good food for you later."

The promise of food was mollifying. Isn't that a great word? Molly, whoever she was, had been such a calming person that if you got calmed or soothed by anything you were mollified. I bet she gave great belly rubs.

Starbuck and I stood sentinel while Atticus picked up all the sidearms, removed the bullets, and put them in a small pile in front of the door. He also had the elemental move the bigger assault rifles underground and sort of puke them up next to the sidearms. He took the ammunition out of those too, and then said we could go.

<We're just going to leave the guys in the ground there, and all those guns piled up?>

"Yep. The scientist guy said he had people to call. It'll be fine. We—or rather you, but thanks for getting me involved—accomplished what we needed to. No reason for us to linger."

<This is the weirdest thing, Atticus. Years of waiting and all I did was lie down in the grass.>

"Nonsense. You led us to the spot and told me when the guy with the mocha would appear. That turned out to be vital. We prevented him from getting shot and kept the facility secure."

<But aren't you curious about why it was necessary?>

"Sure. But these things have a way of revealing themselves later. Just be patient."

As we approached the copse of trees where Atticus had left his rucksack and things, Starbuck's ears perked up.

<Hooves nearby. Not horse though. Coming this way pretty fast.>

<I hear them too,> I said.

Atticus smiled. "I thought it might be her. No one else would have such a talent with animals."

<What? Who?>

A red-haired woman in leathers tanned in browns and greens appeared, driving a chariot pulled by two huge stags.

"Good morning, Siodhachan Ó Suilebháin," she called, using his original Irish name.

"Flidais. Well met," he replied. The Irish goddess of the hunt reined in her stags and dismounted from her chariot. She flashed a grin at him, then turned her attention to me.

"Well done, Oberon. You were the backup plan that worked perfectly."

I wagged my tail at the *well done*, but then froze. <Backup?>

"I had intended to be here myself, but obviously had difficulty arriving in time. You were intended to get the job done if I couldn't, and you performed admirably."

"Would you mind explaining?" Atticus said. "And releasing Oberon from his non-disclosure agreement? He's terrified of being turned into a Chihuahua."

Flidais laughed. "Of course. Oberon, I release you from the vow of secrecy. You may share everything now. But the short version is, that facility is working on something that provides humanity a path out the darkness it's currently in. Years ago in a prophetic trance, Brighid identified this morning–that moment I specified–as a turning point in the world's history. Had you not saved that scientist, things would have become very bleak indeed. She entrusted me to make sure he survived. And I entrusted you to help in case I failed. A good thing I did, too."

<Are you saying that...I saved the future?>

"I think we can say that, yes."

I turned to Atticus. <You understand that I am the best hound ever and this calls for an extraordinary meal?>

He laughed. "I do. We'll find something legendary in Seattle before we go home."

He told Flidais the mercenaries would probably be paralyzed for another hour but he'd never figured out who paid them, and he wasn't sure if they had additional weapons hidden on their person.

"I'll find out. Leave it with me. Go and enjoy your day."

During our run back to Seattle, I was gripped by a slow-rolling revelation. For years, I'd been a key part of making sure the world got better and never realized it. All that time, just loving my Druid and the occasional poodle, snarfing sausage and taking naps, I was unaware how important I was to the branching tree of history. I think the vast majority of people in the world, living their simple lives, are unaware of how important they are. If they love people and the planet, then they're doing the best thing they can possibly do.

Atticus found us a great place in Seattle that served up Wagyu steaks, exquisitely marbled with fat and so very delicious. Love is its own reward, of course, but you know what? Beef is pretty great too.

Okay, yeah, it's *really* great.

THE SPY WHO WROTE PLAYS

You never know what you're going to see at the dog park. I mean: Asses, of course. Uptight humans with nervous little dogs. Unkempt humans blitzed out of their gourds on cannabis or alcohol. Fitness humans wearing designer sportswear and juiced up on supergreen superfoods, sweating excess vitamins out of their pores. And then, just when you think you know what role everyone's playing, it'll change in a second. The uptight humans relax and smile because some other dog gives them love. The stoners reach for a moment of clarity because they want to impress some other human, or at least appear responsible. And the fitness humans will have something chocolate or a hunk of cheese and not give me any, but as long as they look guilty afterwards, I forgive them.

But dogs do this too. We can go from happy to playful to tired in a second, and sometimes tempers flare, or more often it's paranoia, because someone spends so long sniffing your backdoor you feel that they have to be planning a full demolition and renovation of that space and you don't want that at all.

I must have sniffed a little too long at the rear of a Staffordshire terrier—often referred to as a pit bull—but in my own defense I thought I caught a whiff of tuna and I was trying to decide if this was the kind of dog who liked to eat cat food. Maybe he knew what I was thinking and took offense, because he whirled and snapped at me and then...kept coming.

Most dogs don't want a piece of me because size-wise I am close to a great big bear. And I thought surely he couldn't be serious at first because the whirl and snap gets the message across just fine—even humans understand that. But then I thought maybe he *wasn't* playing and if he wasn't, I sure shouldn't, because that's how you get hurt. So we were in it, and I have been in too many fights to let him get position, and he couldn't simply muscle me around like he could with most dogs. I had him on his back with his throat in my teeth in about ten seconds and Atticus was telling me to back off in my head.

<Is he going to back off too?>

Yes. I've made sure of it. He was just afraid of how big you were and how long you were lingering behind him. Let him go and scoot back.

I released him, maybe a tiny bit of blood on my muzzle but I hadn't bitten down hard enough to seriously wound him, and the pit bull scrambled to his feet and retreated in one direction while I went in the other. He went to a Fitness Human, a woman in blue stretchy lycra or polyester or something, who was hollering at him and calling him Caesar and she sounded worried and angry at the same time.

<His name is Caesar? Well, he came and he saw but he didn't conquer,> I said.

Hold still. I'm casting camouflage on you, Atticus said.

<Why?>

To avoid blame and allow a graceful exit.

<Blame? I didn't do anything! He started it and I finished it.>

I know, but she'll try to get me to pay for vet bills or something if she knows you belong to me, so we're going to dodge that.

I felt the tickle of the spell settle along my fur and skin just as the woman looked up from Caesar to cast accusing eyes around at the other humans. "Whose dog is that?" she demanded. She stopped at Atticus. "Is he yours?"

"What dog?" Atticus said, then pointed down to my little Boston terrier buddy, Starbuck, who was sitting at feet. "This one?"

"No, that Irish wolfhound."

"Where?"

"Right over there—hey. Where'd he go?"

Atticus started walking to the gated park entrance with Starbuck following by his side.

Walk, don't run, and meet us at the gate, he told me while the Fitness Human turned her head in every direction, trying to spot me again.

We jogged back home after that and he let the camouflage drop after we were out of sight of the park.

I think a bath is in order, he said. *Blood and dirt will not be welcome in Rose's house.*

<Okay. Do you have a story about someone who suddenly changed who they were like Caesar did?>

Hmm. I think so. I remember someone from the seventeenth century.

<Which century is this one again?>

The twenty-first. So we'd be talking about an episode from three hundred and fifty-eight years ago, if that helps.

<Those are more years than I can count. Were there cars yet?> I asked as we trotted next to Atticus with the noise of cars passing us by on the street.

Atticus started talking to us out loud since no one else was around to hear. "No. This was during the Restoration period in England."

<Ah, so this is an English adventure?>

"More of an afternoon coffee with an Englishwoman in Bruges, a city which is now in Belgium, but at the time was part of the Dutch empire and at war with England. The year was 1666. Shakespeare and Queen Elizabeth were dead and colonialism was making European countries rich—but often at war as they jockeyed for power around the globe. Charles II was king of England, and he was a libertine."

<What is a libertine?> Starbuck asked.

"Someone who isn't especially bound by standards of morality. They tend to do what gives them pleasure with little regard for what other people think. And since the king was like that, it influenced the entire country. His reign was a period marked by sexual profligacy."

<What is profig, prof–that thing?>

"Extraordinary immorality, in this case. He sired twelve illegitimate children. But more importantly for the story I'm going to tell you, he reopened the English theatres after they'd been closed for a decade and women were finally allowed to play women on the stage, unlike Shakespeare's time."

<Oh ho! So is this going to be a story about an famous actress?> I asked.

"In a sense. When I met her, she was a spy."

<Holy shrieking cats on a barbecue, Atticus, I can't wait for this one!>

Soon enough I was in the tub covered in bubbles and sending little groupings of them floating in the air with the swishing of my tail.

<Tell me about the spy!> I said.

My fortuitous investment in coffee during its birth as a trade good has proven to be one of my most profitable over the centuries. It was in 1616 that the Dutch started their first coffee plantations in Java, Indonesia. Fifty years later in 1666 I was in Bruges, part of the Dutch Republic, with a small coffee house of my own. And this Englishwoman with ink-stained fingers became a regular there in July, often speaking in English with different companions, and we became friendly once she knew I spoke English too–though I pretended to be from the country so that she wouldn't ask if we knew the same people. I saw her frequently for a few weeks but then her visits trailed off in August, and I thought she had returned to England. She came in one last time, looking significantly worse, her lips drawn into a thin line of worry, and I asked if I might buy her a cup and sit for a brief chat.

She thanked me and invited me to take a chair. "I don't believe I actually got your name, sir," she said. "Forgive me, my manners have been dreadful."

I replied in an accent that I hoped sounded like something from the north, rather than London. "No, no, worry not. I'm Alistair Peabody, at your service."

"I'm Mrs. Aphra Behn."

"A pleasure. What brings you to Bruges, Mrs. Behn, if I may ask?"

"You may ask, though I'm afraid I can't provide a satisfactory answer. It's some business at which I've failed, and I find myself running low on funds and unsure of my return to England."

"Low on funds?" I said. Coffee was an expensive luxury good at the time, enjoyed only among the elite. She understood that I was wondering why she'd come to my cafe if she was cash-strapped.

"My last insouciant luxury. A desperate attempt to cheer myself in the face of ruin. I've just pawned my jewelry."

"My deepest sympathies. Do you have a plan?"

"I don't think I'm suited for the line of work I'm currently in," she said. "Though I don't know what else I might do for employment."

"Forgive me, but is Mr. Behn unable to provide?"

"He is in fact deceased and therefore profoundly unable to help. I must make my own way."

"Oh. My condolences. You truly have no prospects?"

"None here, I'm afraid. Perhaps in England. Though I am not anxious to return to a city riddled by plague, I have little choice. It appears I must go into debt merely to return and sustain myself."

"Goodness gracious," I said. "I note that your fingers bear evidence of correspondence."

She glanced down and then covered up her right hand self-consciously with her left. "Yes. Arrangements to be made. Petitions for aid."

"Quite. Tell me, have you any love for the theatre?"

"I do."

"I hear there are two companies now with charters from the king."

"Yes, but...Mr. Peabody, I know that women are allowed on stage now thanks to His Majesty, but I am no actress, if that's what you're suggesting."

"Nothing of the sort. I am suggesting that if you have a neat hand, those companies will need a scribe. They require copies of plays, and it's paid work."

"Oh!" She blinked, considering. "That is certainly a possibility. I'm acquainted with the leader of the King's Company, Thomas Killigrew. In fact, I would say he owes me a favour, since it is largely his fault I'm in this situation. And occupying myself as a scribe would be a good deal more wholesome than a number of other unsavoury professions I could pursue."

"There you are. At least one prospect, then, when you return to London."

"Yes. Thank you, Mr. Peabody."

We nattered on about inconsequential things after that until she took her leave, and though I never saw her again, I did learn what became of her afterward.

It turned out she was in Bruges to attempt to turn a man into a double agent for England–the task at which she failed. She'd been recruited to the position by Thomas Killigrew in Antwerp. But she returned to England and became a scribe for both the King's Company and the Duke's Company, and in so doing acquired an education in playwriting that few others enjoyed. She wrote copies of Shakespeare, of course, but also many other playwrights of the age, and her acquaintance with Killigrew and others no doubt provided much inspiration. She eventually began writing her own plays, and the Duke's Company produced most of them.

If you wished to categorize them, they were mostly of a kind now referred to as Restoration Comedies–lots of loose morals and hopping into bed. These were the types of plays that were popular at the time, though she took considerable criticism for writing them when men who served up the same content received no criticism at all. And she replied to that criticism–she didn't merely take it. She pointed out the hypocrisy of men, the unfairness of arranged marriages, the many privileges and abuses of patriarchy, and suggested women should have equal rights. For this she suffered many abuses. But she kept dishing it out. She wrote a poem about male impotence called "The Disappointment," which caused a good deal of impotent male rage. And her play, *The Rover*, was so popular that she had to write a sequel. King Charles II commanded a private performance of it.

One year before her death, she wrote a novel called *Oroonoko*, which is now considered one of the first examples of abolitionist literature and indeed one of the first modern novels.

Because of Aphra Behn, who did so much work carving out a space for women to work in theatre and literature, future playwrights and novelists were allowed to shine. I wish I had known at the time what she would become, but of course there was no way for me to know that the frustrated woman I had coffee with would become so influential and leave such a legacy.

But there is an example of someone who changed who they were to become a completely different person. Though she may have become a spy again for a few years in between plays, and I think she did a much better job that time since we don't know much about what she was up to.

After a quick rinse and towel off, I went outside for zoomies and wondered if I could ever change to become a completely different kind of hound. Perhaps if circumstances demanded it, I could. I mean, I would never like squirrels or stop liking sausage: Those were core values. But maybe I could start eating carrots or something wild like that. I could have Atticus film me eating crunchy vegetables and go viral on social media platforms because apparently there are millions of people who just want to watch animals crunch on things. Not sure what I would get out of that, though, besides fiber.

It's probably best that I don't change—I'm very happy being Oberon. But I understand better now why people have to change very quickly if they want to get along. Atticus changed a lot over the years. I mean, his name used to be Alistair Peabody! And now he's Connor Molloy. And there was that one unfortunate time he was Nigel in Toronto. You never want to be Nigel in Toronto.

I felt bad about making Caesar nervous enough to snap at me and I hoped he wasn't very hurt. He should have all the cat food he wanted if that made him happy. Maybe I could change that about myself: From now on, to keep peace in the universe, I'd spend no longer than three parsecs sniffing another dog's ass, which was way shorter than the Kessel Run and therefore faster than the Millennium Falcon. And incidentally, if I ever got to play monster chess with Chewbacca, I would *not* let the Wookiee win. He's just a great big bear. I can handle great big bears.

I curled up on my bed and sank into a comfy nap with a John Williams soundtrack playing in my head.

MISSISSIPPI DEVIL

Human brains don't work like they should sometimes. Here is how it's supposed to go: What can I eat? What can I play with? What can I hump? Where can I drop a pound or two after I circle around and find the right spot?

See, that's how you live. Right now. But sometimes Atticus will be living in the now and a song or a smell or whatever makes him remember a time in his past and he stops and chews on it–mentally, I mean–and forgets what he was doing, because when he chews on this old memory, it tastes different because so much time has passed. Or it got moldy, I don't know. I really try with my metaphors but I'm not sure I stick the landings.

I get that chewing part, though. You know why hounds will gnaw on bones for a good long while after the meat's all gone? Because there's flavor in there. Undiscovered flavor. And you can find it and taste it if you worry at that bone long enough.

So whenever Atticus kind of freezes in thought, seized by a memory, I privately think he's gone to

Flavor Town. (I mean Memory Flavor Town, not Guy Fieri's Flavortown.)

He froze like that while we were out to lunch. He looked disappointed by the fish and chips he was eating, and that's just the worst. Food should be *good*, and seeing him sad made me sad.

<Atticus, this is so tragic! Why don't we go on a food field trip? Something you haven't had in a long time and we have never had?>

<Yes, new food!> Starbuck said. He was always happy to try things with me and even tried things I warned him about. He insisted on independent confirmation that yucky things were yucky, like cauliflower. When he tried some, I had to turn away and cover my ears so I didn't hear the cruciferous crunching.

<Blech. That's nasty,> he said. <You were right, Oberon.>

"I think a field trip is a good idea," Atticus said. "I was eating these entirely mediocre chips and wishing I had something with real spice, some body to it, but still made with simple ingredients. And I thought of the perfect thing, but it's on the other side of the planet and we can't get there quickly. We'll have to take an Old Way and then probably hitchhike the rest of the way. You'll be in the back of a truck or something and it's going to be a journey. Are you okay with that?"

<Okay with new food? Three kinds of cat shit, Atticus, I can't believe you even have to ask!>

<Yes food!> Starbuck agreed.

So Atticus texted Rose that we were going down to Rosedale and wouldn't be back for a day or two, and we took an Old Way that let us travel from Launceston to Little Rock, Arkansas. The time zone change was pretty extreme, so we went from like noon in

Launceston to nine o'clock the previous night in Arkansas. Then we did indeed have to hitchhike, traveling in the back of a nasty old pickup slimed with chicken shit and mud while Atticus changed his accent and mannerisms to seem like a local as he talked with the driver in the cab.

Rosedale was a city on the border of Mississippi and Arkansas, which meant we had to cross the Mississippi River to get there. We crossed the Helena Bridge, silver moonlight bouncing off the water, and I told Starbuck that the river had catfish in there bigger than me.

<There are catfish? Taste like cat? Meow like cat?>

<They have whiskers like cats. But they taste like fish. Good fish. Especially fried.>

I told Atticus we would need to add fried catfish to the trip for Starbuck's sake and he agreed.

Almost as soon as we got over the bridge into Mississippi, we had our driver drop us off at Highway 1, which trailed south along the river. It was about midnightish, I was guessing, and the driver was nervous about that, asking if we were sure, but Atticus said we'd be okay and thanked him. We started hitching for a new ride down to Rosedale, but there were only like two cars at that time, and neither was inclined to pick up a stranger at night with a huge hound like me and a bonus Boston terrier. About five minutes into our walk, it started raining. Hard.

<We will be dog fish soon,> Starbuck said, shaking himself to get some of the water out of his fur. Atticus knew about a place we could go to wait out the storm, though: There was this place called Moon Lake, which was sort of shaped like a crescent moon on a map, and there was a scenic overlook you could access from the highway. It was a boardwalk that extended out to a roofed pavilion thingy, and there were benches there,

so we jogged to that spot to get out of the rain and wait for the sun. Starbuck and I had a good shake but we were still super wet. Since we had no idea of how long we'd be stuck there, Atticus asked if we'd like a local story to pass the time.

"We can call it a bathtime story if you want, since you're soaked," he said. And we wanted. We got a story in the dark.

Nearly a hundred years ago I was called to this area by the Mississippi elemental, and it was then I first tried the food we're going to have soon. But this story isn't about the food. It's about music and crossroads.

The elemental had felt drains on its energies at a series of crossroads all along what's known today as Old Highway 61, which is just a few miles east of here, running roughly parallel with this road. It had noticed that the drains occurred in a sequence up and down the highway on a fairly regular schedule. If I went to the next crossroads in the pattern, I should be able to witness what was causing the problem.

Crossroads are liminal spaces—by which I mean they are neither here nor there. They are in-between spaces where a choice must be made: You can go forward, change your course to either side, or revisit the road behind. And they invite you to pause and reflect, to look back at past choices and think how you got there and where you want to go next. You also better check if someone is coming fast to intercept you.

And because they're in-between spaces, there's just the tiniest bit of wiggle room for beings of other planes to claim they weren't *really* trespassing. They're a no-man's land where they can confront a man in the midst of making a choice and present him with a truly dangerous one. That's what was happening up and down Highway 61.

A hundred years ago, cars weren't as common as they are now. Lots of people walked for long stretches. And musicians were no exception.

As I sat underneath the shade of a cypress tree, grasshoppers sawing their legs and birds chirping their pleasure about having so many grasshoppers to eat, I watched the crossroads I'd been assigned and saw a Black man approaching from the south, carrying a guitar case. He was in a brown suit with a hat to shade his eyes from the sun, eyes largely downcast but a smile splitting his face, perhaps thinking of a favorite person somewhere.

And then there was suddenly another figure in his path, standing at the crossroads. I hadn't seen him arrive, but I'd been focused on the guitarist. Still, it felt rather abrupt. Suspicious. I carefully got to my feet and cast magical sight, taking a look at both men. The guitarist was human. The man at the crossroads was not.

The latter had an aura of the void about him; he was a creature of hell. Not the being you would call Lucifer or Satan, but a devil of some kind, a demon tasked with corruption.

If I saw such a creature now I would use the gift of Cold Fire that Brighid granted me and unbind him. At that time, however, killing demons was a bit more fraught. I had nothing but my sword and some Druidic blessings. Do enough damage, however, and he'd be unable to maintain his corporeal form on this plane.

I sped up my movements, cast camouflage on myself, and approached, circling somewhat to get behind the demon. As I got closer, I could hear their conversation. The devil was saying in a deep, friendly voice, "Making you a blues legend isn't all I can do, Mr. Robert Johnson. That syphilis you were born with? I can take care of that too."

"No thank you, sir," he said very clearly. "I'm rather attached to my soul and would like to keep it."

I don't know what the devil would have said next. It might have been a threat or something else to sweeten the deal. Regardless, there was no need to save Robert Johnson because he'd already saved himself. Still, there were other people who might be tempted, and this devil had clearly tempted others. Most importantly, that devil had been draining power from Gaia, and that could not be allowed to continue. Without a shred of guilt about being a backstabber–demons don't deserve a fair fight–I shanked him by thrusting Fragarach up into his kidney and just kept going up into his rib cage, figuring I'd hit something vital there.

The devil seized up and a roar erupted from his mouth that was not human. I twisted the blade, the sound ratcheted up a couple of octaves, and he crumbled into oily ashes and polluted the air with the foul stench of brimstone. Mr. Johnson and I both staggered away and retched, though he fell down on his knees, overcome by the strength of his revulsion. I dispelled my camouflage and sheathed my sword, and when Robert Johnson rose from the ground and saw me, he held up a hand defensively.

"Please, sir, don't–"

"I'm not going to hurt you," I said. "I'm sorry I startled you."

"What...what happened?"

"You wisely refused a terrible deal. And I sent that devil back to hell."

"So it *was* the devil."

"He was *a* devil, yes, but maybe not *the* devil."

"And who are you, then, sir, if I may ask?"

"A man who doesn't suffer that kind of thing. That devil has been busy up and down this road. I'm just sorry I didn't get to him sooner. You can call me Calvin Parrish, if you like. Leave out the sir and mister." I extended my hand to shake. "It's an honor to meet you."

My hand pretty much disappeared into his–he had very large hands–and that's when I formally met Robert Johnson.

"You have a sword, Calvin."

"You have a guitar, Robert."

He laughed. "One of those is more common around here than the other."

"True enough. Where you headed?"

"Up to Clarksdale, then back down to Rosedale."

"Okay if I walk with you for a spell?"

"Sure. Let's go. It still stinks here."

And that is how I got to spend a few hours with a blues legend. And when I say legend, I'm not kidding. When I met him, Robert hadn't made a single recording yet. He eventually recorded twenty-nine songs, seven months apart in 1936 and 1937, that have influenced blues and rock ever since. And people came to believe that he sold his soul to the devil at the crossroads to become such a good performer. But he didn't need any help to be great.

The truth is he just took a year or so to learn how to play with a man named Ike Zimmerman. Robert was simply a talented, creative man. And he used that talent to make a living as an itinerant performer. Like many other Delta bluesmen, he traveled up and down Highway 61 and elsewhere, performing in small joints and often on street corners, making an extremely modest living from his art. It was enough to get by during the Great Depression, and he was a rambler–he had girlfriends in most of the towns he visited, and often stayed with them rather than spending money on lodgings.

He died in 1938 at only 27 years old, and there's some mystery about the cause of death, which only fed into the idea he must have sold his soul to the devil, and the devil came to collect. But he did have congenital syphilis, and perhaps Marfan syndrome, which would explain his large hands and maybe hid some heart and circulatory problems. Some folks think he was poisoned by the jealous lover of one of his many girlfriends. Whatever the cause, the world was poorer for his leaving it. I heard his recordings in 1939, and recognized "Cross Road Blues," which he wrote while we walked together and contained absolutely zero mention of the devil. I think perhaps he was still too shaken by the experience to address it directly. He did write "Me and the Devil Blues" and "Hellhound on My Trail" later, but they didn't mention him making a deal either, because of course he never made one.

It is an absolute fact that deals were made with other folks at those crossroads up and down Highway 61, and you can be sure that Robert visited them all and looked for rides at each one. But all the crossroads that claim they're the one where he made his deal are absolute horseshit except for the fact that once upon a time, Robert Johnson had been there, living his life and contributing so much to music history.

Now, one of the songs that he recorded referred to the food we're going to enjoy down in Rosedale: Hot tamales. As Robert wrote, "They're Red Hot." They're not the traditional sort of tamales from Mexican cuisine: the Mississippi Delta region has their own version and I can guarantee you won't be bored with your food the way I was in Tasmania. Robert introduced me to them and whenever I'm in Mississippi I have to have some. There are two main differences between Mississippi hot tamales and traditional ones: First, they're made with cornmeal instead of masa, and second, they're boiled instead of steamed. The fillings vary–you can find pork, chicken, or beef–and the spice levels vary too, but we're going to a small place that's widely regarded as one of the best. It's a house, basically, and the menu has one item on it: Joe's hot tamales. They're actually Barbara's hot tamales now, since Joe passed away a while back and his sister took over, but Joe's name is still on the house.

Robert and I enjoyed some hot tamales together in Clarksdale, and then we parted ways. I only found out I'd been walking with a legend years later. Every so often I spend a few days bathed in blues music and it renews me somehow. Not sure how it accomplishes that, but it works.

The rain stopped soon after Atticus finished but we didn't bother to move; the frogs started croaking, owls and other night birds called, and we napped until dawn. At sunrise we made our way down to Rosedale, walking on the damp muggy roadside for a while, eventually catching a ride in the back of a farmer's truck.

The hot tamales at the White Front Cafe in Rosedale are made with seasoned ground brisket and cornmeal, then wrapped in a cornhusk, tied, and boiled. Atticus bought two dozen for us to share and poured some extra hot sauce on his and washed it down with Dr. Pepper.

I'm not going to say they were better than sausage–I mean, cornmeal isn't necessarily a hound's favorite thing–but I did like them. What I liked most about them was seeing how happy Atticus was. His eyes rolled in pleasure and he made moaning sounds and *that* is how you're supposed to enjoy your food. It was clearly as good as he'd hoped, well worth the time spent and distance crossed, and it beat the ever-loving heck out of cauliflower.

On our way back to Little Rock we stopped somewhere to get fried catfish for Starbuck and he agreed that it was excellent and thankfully tasted nothing like cats. Back in Launceston, Atticus listened to blues music for a few days after we got home and I noticed how his mood seemed generally improved. That was a thing music could do for humans that it didn't do for hounds, and I don't understand its mysterious power except to acknowledge that it's real. He chewed on that music, I guess, and found some new flavor in it. I like it when people enjoy their things.

THE THINKER

I think it must be hard to be a human sometimes. For one thing, they have extremely limited options when it comes time to eliminate bodily wastes. They build entire rooms dedicated to it and have laws—written and unwritten—about where it's okay to do it. And there's that whole cleanup business afterward too, which consumes quite a few resources. Hounds are allowed to do it anywhere but inside the house. We have so *many* options, and it's efficient and really pleasant to sniff around for a good spot, circle around it, and drop a bomb. And then humans clean up after us too, so that's just more work for them and I think it wears them down after a while.

And that's just *one thing* that stresses them out. They have so many other stresses, like the twin evils of insurance companies and leaf blowers. I may have heard something about taxes too, but sometimes people admit taxes do good stuff like pay for fire departments and roads and sewers—the latter being a really important part of their rooms where they dispose of waste. But nobody likes insurance companies or leaf blowers.

I worry about Atticus when he gets stressed and does one of those big sighs. He busted out a long-suffering one after he had a short but tense conversation with Granuaile, who apparently asked him to do something for her.

<What's the matter, Atticus?> I asked him when the sigh trailed away.

"We have to go to France. An elemental has asked for help there and Granuaile is already involved in another long-term project, which means it's up to us. I'm not mad or anything–I'm always happy to help Gaia. I'm just frustrated by the timing. I was hoping to start work on something else."

<Oh, I know that feeling! Sometimes I'm hoping to take a nap and then a squirrel comes along–>

<No squirrel!> Starbuck said. My little Boston terrier buddy leapt and spun in the air, landing solidly on his paws afterward. He'd been doing that ever since he watched the Olympics. <I can pull off one sixteenth of a Simone Biles move,> he explained when I asked him why he did that. <It's called the Starbuck Twist Spin Rotation Thing. It's not good enough to win a gold medal, but I should at least get a snack.>

If I tried to do that I'd probably break something, so I agreed that it was snackworthy.

<Will this errand in France keep you from doing what you wanted to do?> I asked.

"No, I can do it later. I need to shrug it off because my plan was to help Gaia and this will be helping, so I'm really sticking to my plan, just elsewhere. You know what would make me forget all about my frustration, though? A bit of sausage tucked into a real croissant."

Real croissants, apparently, were not easily found in Tasmania. Not that I really cared, because he'd said the magic word: *sausage.*

<I embrace this new plan, Atticus, one billion percent. Where in France are we going?>

"Paris. They tried to clean up the Seine River ahead of the Olympics and made some headway but didn't quite get it done. Pretty far from done, actually, since some athletes who swam in it got extremely sick. The elemental was hoping they'd do a better job, and now that the Olympics are over, time and money that went to cleanup efforts is drying up. And apparently there's a new polluter upriver that we need to find and eliminate—they were waiting for attention to be directed elsewhere and have been dumping some kind of sludge in there."

<More food, less sludge!> Starbuck said.

"I just need to tell Rose that we're headed out and then we can go," he said, pulling out his phone and starting to tap at it with his thumb. Now that he had committed to the project, his attitude had rebounded and he even sounded a bit excited. I think that was a testament to the healing power of sausage.

But we didn't leave right away because of time zones. Morning in Tasmania was the dank heart of darkness in France. We had to wait for the afternoon before leaving so that we would arrive in Paris when the bakeries opened with hot fresh croissants. We ate only a little bit so we'd still be hungry when we got there, and whoa dang were we ever! Especially when we smelled all that breakfast.

Walking there got us even more worked up because we did our traveling via Old Ways now and it was always a bit of a journey. But it was worth it: After all that building of expectations, Atticus didn't go to a boulangerie or patisserie at all for a croissant, but rather took us to a street food vendor that sold something called a galette saucisse. There are a lot of variations regarding the toppings and preparation, but it's basically a buckwheat crepe rolled around a hot grilled sausage with a bit of melted cheese and let me tell you, it might be the best idea the French ever had, and rumor has it the French have had a lot of ideas regarding food. (Not all of them are good: Snails, for example, are undelicious. But have a galette saucisse just one time and you can forgive them for the snail thing.)

Being in Paris was a little strange for Starbuck and me because we were in a country that spoke a different language, so we were unable to understand most of the humans around us and it was like being a regular dog walking around with Atticus. Judging by tone and expression, however, they were saying things humans usually say: I am very large and handsome (très grand et beau), and Starbuck is very small and cute (très petit et mignon). Atticus says that these are compliments, but we understand that they are facts. I got called "magnifique" a lot and I can't disagree.

When we got to the River Seine, Atticus warned us not to drink any of it or even get it in our mouths, but we were okay to just wade in the shallows and keep our paws wet. He waded in too and then he looked like he was going to start talking to the elemental through his magic tattoos and everything, so I stopped him before he could zone out.

<Atticus, wait.>

"What is it?"

<This is going to take a long time, right? And we're wet, so it technically counts as a bath. So you have to tell us a story.>

"Oberon, I have to concentrate."

<No, don't give me that! You have a buttload of headspaces. I know you can talk to the elemental and us at the same time. Tell us a story so we won't be worried that we're standing in a river full of bacteria and chemicals.>

"What kind of story do you want?"

Starbuck shouted before I could reply, <We get a cow chef who feeds us beef forever!>

<Something about why humans are stressed and how they deal with it,> I said.

"What? Oberon, are you stressed?"

<No, I'm très magnifique. I just want to understand humans more.>

"Hmm." Atticus thought for a minute before he said, "I think I've got it. Okay, here we go."

A couple hundred years—no, I must go further back. Seven hundred-ish years ago in Italy, a man named Dante Alighieri wrote a trio of epic poems that are known as The Divine Comedy. In my opinion, they are simultaneously legitimate works of beauty and genius and also one of the single greatest sources of stress and suffering in the world. The first one, in particular, is still widely read today: it's called *Inferno*, and it describes in detail nine levels of hell and the punishments assigned to the damned on each level. It's graphic and gruesome and has penetrated the popular imagination so well that most people don't realize that it bears little relationship to the Bible. There are no levels of hell or purgatory listed in the Bible. All that came from Dante. And most other popular ideas of hell that didn't come from him came from Milton's *Paradise Lost*.

Humans are hardwired to think about the future because we want to avoid danger, and if we can foresee threats to our survival, maybe we can dodge them or at least minimize our risk. Which means we think ahead, and that often has drawbacks but again, the benefit is that we avoid an early death. Indeed, we try to avoid that as long as we can–I've arguably been more successful at that than almost anyone. A major source of worry or stress for us is the question of when we'll die and what happens when we do. Dante provided a detailed answer of one possibility: An eternity of torment in return for an all-too-brief seventy or so years on earth–if you were lucky. That fear of hell gripped all of Europe and later, its colonies. Centuries of a certain kind of preacher telling stories about damnation wreaked havoc on the collective unconscious–at least in the parts of the world dominated by Christianity. But it also inspired some rather impressive art.

Skip forward six hundred years or so to nineteenth-century France. I was in the country for a while in 1888, moving around from place to place. Vincent Van Gogh, one of the world's most famous painters, was in Arles, producing some of his most celebrated works like *The Bedroom* and *Café Terrace at Night*, and he cut off his ear in December of that year after a quarrel with another painter, Paul Gaugin, who was staying in the same house as he was. But here in Paris, a man named Auguste Rodin was creating the world's most famous sculpture after he read nothing but Dante for a year.

Rodin's immersion in The Divine Comedy inspired him in 1880 to embark on a massive project called *The Gates of Hell*, described in the first part of *Inferno*. It's a huge work and we can go see it later if you like. It has two hundred different figures or elements worked into it, and several of them were cast independently and became famous sculptures in their own right. The most famous of these is now known as *The Thinker*, but when he began to work on it in 1888, it was known as *The Poet*–referring to Dante. Rodin placed Dante above the gates, looking down on the levels of hell, contemplating the ruin and despair of the damned. But this was no pale, skinny figure who spent his life in sedentary thought: Rodin's Thinker was packed with muscle, all of it tense and coiled, ready to spring into action if the thoughts he was thinking demanded it.

He represents, to many, the complete package: Intellect combined with physical strength. And the naturalism of Rodin's work–far more realistic than the idealized forms of earlier artists–influenced a generation of sculptors. But it was also out of sync with his contemporaries: at this time France was wading in the lily-pad ponds of Claude Monet and the Impressionists, and here was an artist saying no, let's look at the rude reality of existence and confront the problems of being human.

I met Rodin at a boxing match when he had come to ask one of the fighters, Jean Baud, to model for him. Boxing has been a sport as long as I've been alive, but it was enjoying an upswell of interest in the late Victorian era. I liked to dip my toes in and out of the sport, see how things were going, keep myself sharp, and test myself in the ring unaided by Gaia. I didn't fight for prizes, you understand: I would go to gyms and ask to spar. That's how I met Jean Baud. He'd taught me a couple of moves and I taught him more than a couple. But when Rodin approached and introduced himself, I had no idea who he was.

At the time he was forty-eight, I think, with a long full beard and a flat cap. He took a brief look at me but had come to see Jean since he'd just won a fight. And Jean, to be fair, was a bit thicker and more well-muscled than me.

Rodin explained that he was an artist and that he'd pay Jean to model for him a few hours a day as Rodin worked in clay. Getting reliable pay as a boxer was difficult, so Jean readily agreed.

My interest was piqued because most sculptors at the time didn't work in clay. It was too temporary a medium; it quickly deteriorated without firing. But Rodin would sculpt quickly and then his assistants would create plasters and casts from his original clay work.

I asked if I could attend the first sitting and Rodin objected almost without thinking, but relented when I offered to pay his fee to Jean. That is how I got to see his studio at what is now the Musée Rodin, but which was a hotel at the time. I saw *The Gates of Hell* in process and watched him maul and shape some clay into the early form of *The Thinker*. It was clear that he was going to leave quite a legacy, and though we had very little conversation, I felt blessed to witness the inception of one of the world's most famous works of art.

And someone else was there: Camille Claudel, a genius sculptor in her own right. I had no inkling of the tempestuous relationship she had with Rodin and did not learn of her fate until many years later. She was committed to an asylum, apparently by her mother and her brother, Paul, and kept there for thirty years until her death despite the asylum staff repeatedly telling the family that she was fine to be released. I have strong suspicions—but no solid proof—that Paul

Claudel may have been a legendary asshole. He only visited his sister seven times in thirty years and allowed her to be buried in an unmarked common grave.

Rodin never fully finished *The Gates of Hell*, despite working on it until his own death. The first bronze casting of it in its nearly complete form was begun just a few weeks before he died. Looking back on it now, I think that both he and Claudel were doing their best to wrestle with their inner demons and defeat them. I cannot say for sure that either of them won. But I am absolutely sure that they both did their best: You can see their struggles come alive in their work.

Atticus chuckled after he finished. "I'm not sure what insight that might have provided into humans. If we were capable of figuring ourselves out, the world wouldn't be like this."

<You mean a polluted river and galette saucisse in the same city? The horrible and the wonderful existing side by side?>

"Yes. That's humanity for you," Atticus agreed.

<Except that's going on in your heads too?>

"I think so, yes. I mean, plenty of us want to clear out the horrible bits and work at it pretty hard, whether it's through religion or therapy or spa days or whatever. But the darkness is always there, in one way or another."

<I can't imagine what that's like.>

"Okay. Uh...imagine that your brain is full of sausage and poodles."

<I don't have to imagine that. It *is* full of sausage and poodles! Speaking of which, are we going to see any French ones?>

"Hold on, don't get distracted. If you were a human, it wouldn't be just sausage and poodles in your head. There would also be squirrels and cats and great big bears."

Starbuck and I were so offended by this that we leapt out of the water and barked at him. I have never heard anything so rude in my life! And you know what he did? He *laughed.*

"I think you understand why humans are often stressed now," he said. "We have a lot to deal with in our heads. Some of it was already in there, just part of the operating system we can't delete. But lots of it is garbage put in there by someone else, and taking out the metaphorical trash is a chore we need to perform constantly or we'll have brains that look like a hoarder's house, cluttered and moldy and diseased."

<How...how do you deal with it?> Starbuck asked.

"I travel the world with my friends and give them belly rubs," Atticus replied. "It's very relaxing."

<You...hey! He means us!> Starbuck said.

<Promise you'll give us one when you're finished?> I asked. <It's for your own good.>

"I promise," he replied, and that was very pleasing. Starbuck and I curled up on the riverbank for a nap while he worked. I had delightful dreams of a French poodle named Élodie who gave me a dozen galettes saucisse and then let me chase her through a field of heather. Ah, Élodie, ma belle fille!

Okay: je suppose que je connais un peu le français. Juste un petit peu.

THE SKINNY DIPPER

You know how sometimes you get a good bone and it has some really nice meat and fat on it and you nibble and gnaw on it and it keeps buzzing the pleasure center of your brain so that you get obsessed with it and keep going and going the way this sentence keeps going and going? I have a lot of experience with this because Atticus is super nice to me and gives me more bones than the average hound. Now I've never seen humans go after bones the way dogs do, but I think most of you can relate to this metaphor because I've overheard you talk about good bones you've had and you close your eyes when you remember it and say things like "Oh, *damn*, it was so good." But for me–and lots of dogs and humans–it's getting to the past tense that's difficult. Because when you have a good bone, you don't want to stop enjoying it. You just keep at it and then you think about it constantly and it's tough to let it go.

It gets to feel pretty strange when you have all the good stuff off the bone and you know it doesn't actually taste good anymore but you can't stop because you remember it how good it used to be and your brain just wants more of that thing. Atticus says when brains do this it's a sign of either addiction or obsession, which are related but are not exactly the same. Professional brain people have a complete grasp of the nuances but Atticus knew enough to guess that my thing about bones was an obsession.

<Is it bad to be obsessed?> I asked him.

"It can be. But it can also lead to tremendous breakthroughs–the history of science is full of obsessed people. I'd say that while some obsessions can lead to problems, plenty of them are harmless. I was obsessed with capybaras for a while. Had a little collection of capybara sculptures until I got over it."

<Hmm. I don't know that my obsession with bones is going to lead to any breakthroughs, Atticus. I'm worried that it's the bad kind of obsession."

"If you liking bones was worrisome, you could depend on me to tell you. There is nothing to worry about, Oberon, trust me."

My Boston terrier buddy, Starbuck, had been listening and chose that moment to demonstrate his mastery of a newly acquired Australian expression: <No worries, mate!>

<Well, Atticus, can you give me an example of how someone's harmless obsession became a good thing? Like, from history?>

"You mean like a quick example, or are you wanting a story?"

"I want a story, but I don't want a bath."

"Okay. How about a compromise? Let's go to the Cataract Gorge and swim in the basin, and I'll tell you a story there."

<Yes, swim!> Starbuck said, spinning around in excitement. <No worries, mate! Smell you later!>

We'd been to Cataract Gorge several times before. There's a swimming pool nearby for humans who like to have a lifeguard around and chemically treated water, but you can swim in the gorge itself for free at this big hole in the South Esk River. Atticus keeps us on a leash until we get to the water and he steers us away from everyone so they're not bothered by us and we're not bothered by them. Both Starbuck and I like to take running jumps into the water and make big splashes, and sometimes when tiny humans see me coming their way at full speed they scream and fill their diapers, so we try to avoid that.

We charged the pool and dove in, splashing around in the coolness for a while. Once you're in the basin you see cliff faces all around with trees for hair. The water has no sharks or krakens or shrieking eels, which are my preferred swimming conditions. Then we swam over to shore where Atticus was sitting on a boulder and shook ourselves to get him all wet. He knew it was coming and bore it patiently.

"Ready now?" he asked.

<Yes, story!> Starbuck said.

<It's a beautiful day for a story about obsession,> I agreed. <Please proceed.>

This took place almost exactly two hundred and one years ago in Washington, D.C. It was 1823, and the United States had just recently acquired Florida from the Spanish and expanded its territorial claims all the way to the Pacific Northwest due to the Adams-Onís Treaty. This was pretty big news at the time and I heard about it and thought it was remarkable statecraft.

That is because the Secretary of State back then was John Quincy Adams, serving under President Monroe. He was a man given to obsession, much like his father, John Adams.

John Adams was the second president of the United States—what the Americans call a Founding Father—and after his single term, he developed an obsession with making sure his son eventually became president too. He passed on much of his intensity and obsessive nature to his son, but it manifested much differently in Quincy, if we may call him that.

Quincy was obsessed with schedules and personal health. He wrote in a journal pretty much daily from age 12 until his death. He woke up every day at the same time, and then he went for a swim in whatever body of water was closest—a pond, river, ocean, it didn't matter—but he did so in the nude. He was firmly convinced of its health benefits, and while jumping into some cold water and back out again has been shown to provide some vascular and circulatory advantages, being naked wasn't really a factor. Still, he didn't know that. He just knew it was good for him and he was determined to reap his healthy rewards on schedule.

And he was not shy if other people were around. I don't mean he was an exhibitionist: he never sought people out so he could disrobe in front of them. He merely had a schedule to maintain, and if someone had the misfortune to be nearby when he wanted his early morning swim, he wasn't going wait for them to leave. He just shucked himself free of the tyranny of pants and went for it.

Later this was used against him when he became president—that was a year later. He used to go down to the Potomac River most mornings for his swim, and one day an enterprising woman working as a journalist took his clothes and wouldn't give them back until he agreed to an interview.

I did something similar, seeing an opportunity to talk to a man who was in a unique position to influence the course of history. If there was a chance for me to influence him without using magic and tipping off Aenghus Óg to where I was, so much the better.

Usually I avoid getting involved in politics and this turned out to be a good example of why: It's difficult to notch a clear win. You're never sure you can craft a policy that will achieve your desired outcomes because it often gets changed or watered down on its way into law, and the ripple effects years down the road from a mutant hybrid bill can be unexpected.

I felt it was worth taking the risk, so knowing that Quincy liked his morning swims, I methodically frequented some swimming holes near his place until I found him and asked if I could join. He said sure, so I stripped down and dove in.

My tattoos were an immediate topic of conversation and I used my American accent because believe it or not, there was a fair amount of distrust of the Irish at that time. We were still about twenty years before the potato famine, but Irish immigrants were already unwelcome in America.

"I can't say I've ever seen tattoos like that," Quincy said.

"Don't be alarmed," I replied, "but I'm a pagan. A friendly and peaceful one who enjoys the rejuvenating effects of wild bathing."

"A pagan, you say? Extraordinary. I haven't met many."

"There are more than you might realize. They tend not to advertise it since there can be repercussions."

We hadn't introduced ourselves and I had no intention of doing so. I wanted to keep up the pretense that we were just two citizens who happened to like swimming, not the Secretary of State and an ancient Druid.

"But you're local? You grew up here?"

"No, I'm originally from Ireland, but I've been here a good while now."

"Fascinating. Have you traveled much, then?"

"It's safe to say I've seen a good portion of the world, yes."

"Excellent. Do you speak any other languages?"

"More than the average, I'd wager."

"Russian, perhaps?"

"Da."

Quincy had spent several years as the minister to Russia and spoke it well, so he switched to that language.

"How long were you there?" he asked, and I was intentionally vague. I couldn't tell him that I had spent a few years on and off in different centuries–the first time was with the generals of Genghis Khan who invaded the Rus' tribes about six hundred years earlier. I had participated in the Battle of Kalka River under command of Subutai, who was in my opinion the greatest military commander the world has ever known–but that's a different story.

I told him, "Just a few years," leaving out the details. "But they're becoming an issue, aren't they?"

"Russia? How so?"

"Well. I don't mean to ruin a perfectly good swim with world politics, but if you look at how Russia, Austria, and Prussia are eyeing this half of the world as ripe for picking, you can see how it would be alarming, especially to people in the west."

"How is this half ripe?"

"The Spanish are falling apart over here. Look at that clever deal Adams made, securing Florida and expanding US territory to the west as well."

Quincy snorted, amused that I apparently didn't know who I was talking to. "Clever indeed."

"Right, so Russia is feeling full of themselves since they stomped on Napoleon at Waterloo. Perhaps they took a moment to consider the hoards of wealth the Spanish, English, French, and Portuguese accrued over here and thought they wouldn't mind filling their own coffers. They made that proclamation a couple of years ago laying claim to Alaska and the Pacific Northwest. But allowing new colonial powers to exert their influence over here will only lead to war and costly security measures in the future. Best to help the Spanish lose their grip where we can and prevent others from getting involved. It's clearly in the nation's security interests to discourage other powers from exerting influence in this hemisphere, but thus far it's not been expressed. One can only hope Adams is seeing that clearly and will do something about it soon."

He stopped swimming and frowned at me. I'd probably overstepped with that and aroused his suspicions. The common man was not so concerned with foreign affairs.

"Do you work for the Federal government?" he asked, switching back to English.

"No. I'm an herbalist who imports rare herbs from around the globe to craft salubrious salves, teas, and tonics for a variety of agues and ill humors. As such, I'm selfishly interested in preventing wars with powers that have better navies than the United States."

"That would be quite nearly everyone at this point."

I chuckled. "Indeed."

"Declaring that other countries should leave this hemisphere alone would be unenforceable."

"For the moment, yes. But we can build up a navy to enforce it later. Stating the policy will allow future administrations the chance to enforce it when the navy materializes, and in the meantime other powers might enforce it for us."

"Other powers?"

"Well, I imagine the British. They'd like to keep other colonial powers out of the New World because it might interfere with their ongoing looting or, if we're being polite, trade. All these new countries south of the border declaring their independence from Spain are new markets for the British to exploit."

"We must be polite, sir."

"Quite right, my apologies. Let me say, then, that Britain's trade interests will encourage it to support the United States' position, should it ever be articulated."

Quincy laughed at that and resumed his swim. The conversation was essentially over, and I'd said my piece. I finished up my swim and bade him good fortune and good health. Months later, President James Monroe uttered what came to be known as the Monroe Doctrine, authored by John Quincy Adams. It said that the United States would not support any further European colonialism in the western hemisphere while pledging to leave Europe alone. And it was absolutely unenforceable until after the Civil War, when there was an actual navy capable of doing something. Even then it got selectively enforced, to be sure, and corollaries and additions to it made it a convenient tool in the twentieth century to allow the United States to conduct all sorts of shenanigans, like annex Hawai'i.

So it has become a very questionable thing over two hundred years. Had Monroe not stated the United States' position against new colonial interference in the Americas, we might have Russian colonies on the west coast. We might have had unceasing war between colonial powers in all of the Americas throughout the nineteenth century. Instead we got some sporadic wars and Manifest Destiny and the genocide of indigenous peoples. There's no way for me to judge it as a good thing, you see. Just a suspicion that if it hadn't been made, events might have turned out far worse.

And there's no way I can know in advance when I do things like that. I certainly didn't see Hawai'i coming. The only thing I can be fairly sure of is that I'll be around to experience the ripples of whatever I do, and I don't want to cock things up, so I tend to stay out of politics.

But that swim I had with John Quincy Adams was only possible because of his obsession with what came to be known as skinny dipping. He pretty much made it a popular practice.

Sometimes, if you know someone's obsession, you can meet them where they're at and get something real done. I don't know for certain that the Monroe Doctrine would never have been written without me, but I do know I added a nudge to the mountain of evidence that Adams was no doubt facing that something needed to be said about colonial meddling in the New World. I hope it was a net positive compared to the alternatives, but I can't ever truly know one way or the other."

I'm glad Atticus doesn't meddle with human politics very much. From what I can tell, it sounds like more than half the people involved in it shout very bad ideas to the public on a consistent basis and then ask for money so they can turn their bad ideas into bad policies. Starbuck had a question.

<So is skinny dipping good?>

"Depends on where you do it. If you do it in some places in South America, for example, there are parasites in rainforest rivers that can swim up inside of your penis and cause all sorts of unpleasantness."

<Let's never go there,> he said, laying his ears back. <Let's stay here.>

<Your story was very nice, Atticus, and congratulations on getting naked with a U.S. President, but it didn't really help me with my problem, especially since you don't even know if what you did was a good thing. How do I turn my obsession with bones into a net positive? Do you think a cinnamon-coated poodle from Spain named Dulce de Leche will walk by as I'm gnawing on a beef rib and say, "Oh my, Oberon, you have such a very big bone!" and I'll feel proud of it and then we'll go skinny dipping in a river with water so clear you can see the parasites?>

"That's a lot to unpack, Oberon, but I'm impressed with your rich fantasy life. Honestly, I don't think you have to worry–"

<No worries, mate!> Starbuck interrupted.

"Right. Because you are already a net positive. Enjoy your bones. They're delicious and should be enjoyed. And this day should be enjoyed too. Want to swim again? I'll join you this time."

Starbuck and I wagged our tails and stood as he peeled off his shirt. He fell backward into the water and then floated on his back. Starbuck and I trotted away from the shore and then got a running start so we could jump in on either side of him and splash him good.

He laughed and we had the best time. Bones and poodles are great, but having fun with my Druid friend is my favorite obsession.

SEEKING HARMONY

Sometimes I like it when you have no choice. Like when you go to that café in *My Cousin Vinny* and the only thing on the menu is Breakfast, and you're like, yeah, I'll have that then. Easy! No stress.

Because sometimes you have too many choices. Like when Atticus took us to a butcher shop in Tasmania and paid the guy extra to let me and Starbuck in to check out the offerings. There were more than seventy-five billion sausages in there behind glass, a figure that you should not trust at all because I lose count after twenty and just make things up, and Atticus said we could have just two of them, but we had to choose.

There was pork sausage, beef sausage, chicken and turkey sausage, and each kind had their own varieties of flavors. I mean, chicken apple is normally my go-to, but there were sausages I'd never had before! Shouldn't I at least try them? But what if they weren't very good and I passed up chicken apple for something mediocre? I suddenly had all this stress. What if I chose wrong? I mean, in one sense I couldn't lose because the best sausage is always the one in front of you, but in another sense, it was possible that out of four thousand sausages, I would pick the worst two!

<Gaaah! Atticus, all this wurst is the worst!>

Why? he asked. *You can have any two sausages you want.*

<But I'm being pulled in so many directions! Do I go for the Bourbon Swiss pork sausage or the Beefheart Apocalypse or the Chicken Apple Festival or the Turkey Bacon Bomb or, you know, all these others? It's too much!>

<Too much good stuff!> Starbuck agreed. <But I'll have the Bacon Cheddar Carnival and the Sultry Sinner Sausage.>

<Three kinds of cat shit, Starbuck, what the heck is that?>

<I don't know. I'm going to find out!>

<Atticus, what if those are the best? What if I miss my chance to get the best possible sausage in this situation?>

Oberon, you've taken what many would consider a luxury and turned it into a burden. The fact that you get to make a choice at all is a tremendous blessing.

<But haven't you ever been pulled in many directions like this? You understand, right? It would be like a cheeseburger yodeling to you on the left and a plate of hot wings on the right, crooning that their hearts will go on like Celine Dion.>

That's too mushy for hot wings. If you're looking for sentiment with an edge, I think they would sing "Home Sweet Home" by Motley Crüe. But I do know what you mean. I have a story about someone who was pulled in many directions, in fact. Ironically, he was studying things being pulled in many directions, but didn't see that he was one of them.

<You mean like being drawn and quartered? I've heard about that, which makes no sense because the person really isn't quartered.>

What?

<If you pull off the arms and legs from a person you still have the body. That's a fifth piece. So it should be drawn and, uh. Quinted.>

That's not a word, Oberon.

<I still deserve an extra sausage for my creativity.>

<Hey, me too!> Starbuck said. <I deserve an extra sausage because of...my ears! They're shapely. Rose said so.>

Nice try, but no extra sausages, just the two. Pick two sausages, Oberon, that are different from Starbuck's. Then, if you both agree, we will halve each sausage and divide them equally, which means you each get to try four different sausages today. Some other day we can try four more until you have tried them all and know which ones are best.

Starbuck and I both liked that plan, so I picked the Bourbon Swiss and the Beefheart Apocalypse. When we got home and tried them, it turned out that the ones with cheese in them were the best—the Bourbon Swiss and the Bacon Cheddar Carnival. The Apocalypse was dry and poorly spiced, and the Sultry Sinner Sausage was an affront to taste and common decency, as it had something in it that tasted like black licorice.

After that I remembered that Atticus had a story for us, but it sounded like a bathtime thing and we weren't really dirty.

"Go outside for a few minutes and get dirty, then," he said.

A command to get dirty when usually he told us to keep clean? Yes, sir! Starbuck and I played in the backyard and wriggled around in the dirt underneath the deck. Little puffs of it poofed from our coats as we walked, and Atticus made a strangled sound in his throat when he saw us come in like that.

"Okay, that's the last time I tell you to do that," he said. "Go get in the tub."

<Both of us at the same time?>

"Yes. Let's do this."

Starbuck and I trotted in there and leapt into the tub, which was called a clawfoot model but honestly, it didn't have real claws. More like silver feet. Atticus hosed us down and got started.

Johannes Kepler was a man trained to give astrological horoscopes, and I met him in Prague in 1601. Astrology was considered to be a serious thing back then–and of course, many people still take it seriously today. But owing in part to Kepler, Galileo, Isaac Newton, and others, this was the time when astrology began to tilt toward pseudo-science while astronomy was gradually getting married to physics. I spent much of those decades bopping around Europe talking to astronomers and physicists, because they had something to teach me. Galileo, I think I've mentioned before, was a particular genius that I've admired for a long time.

In England, Queen Elizabeth was still attending the plays of Shakespeare. People were dealing with plague and fires and cholera, but at the same time, all the sciences were beginning to flourish. Kepler was also trained in mathematics and astronomy and it was to these fields, as well as optics, that he made significant contributions. He's been described as the last great astrologer and the first great astronomer. But it wasn't just the push and pull of astronomy and astrology that troubled him; it was also the opposite energies of science versus religion. He wanted to explain the natural world in terms of God's plan; his drive to understand it, like many scientists of his day, was to understand the language of God. It was a particular tension because science demanded accuracy and proof, but there was the problem of making that work with the Biblical worldview, which was...less than scientific. Lots of it had to be accepted on faith. And disagreeing with the Bible could get you in significant trouble back then, as Galileo and many others found out.

The old Biblical belief was that the sun and stars and everything orbited the earth. Copernicus, Galileo, and others said no, the earth and all the planets orbit the sun. But in the Copernican system, the planets orbited the sun in a perfect circle, and that was not true.

Figuring that out and identifying that orbits were elliptical was Kepler's great triumph, but he was only able to discern that thanks to the detailed measurements of Mars's orbit taken by Tycho Brahe, a Danish astronomer who had an observatory near Prague. You would have liked Tycho. He had a magnificent blonde mustache that drooped from either side of his upper lip like two tails of yellow labrador retrievers.

I met both men in Prague in 1601, though spent much more time speaking with Kepler. Brahe died later that year of a bladder infection, but his observations on Mars were key to Kepler unlocking the mysteries of planetary orbits.

Kepler and I sat at an underground pub that no longer exists after Brahe departed on some business elsewhere in the city. I'd told both of them that I was a scientist from Ireland, which they believed because I had the accent, of course, and appeared to know what they were talking about. As was customary for me whenever traveling in Christian lands, I wore long sleeves and a glove on my right hand to conceal my tattoos, but I usually lied and said it was to conceal unsightly scars.

Kepler was a dark-haired individual with a neatly trimmed beard. Unlike the majority of people in Prague, he was a Lutheran–another source of tension for him. And this led him to inquire whether I might think less of him for it, as the Irish he'd heard of were typically Catholic.

"Not at all," I told him, and then took a risk, because it might end the conversation. "Would you think less of me if I were not Christian?"

He nearly spat his drink. His eyes bulged. "What? You're...what?"

"A pagan. I can pretend well enough and make Christian noises to get along in the world, but my gods are not the jealous sort or the kind to demand martyrdom, so they don't mind if I give the lie as I make my way through Christendom."

"Why are you telling me this?"

"Because we are men of science. We seek the truth of things, and we can hardly do that if we are not truthful with one another. And of course, I wish to make the point that people of all faiths have a deep and abiding interest in solving the mysteries of the earth and the skies."

"There are so many!" he said, and I heartily agreed. Our conversation ranged widely from that point and touched on many subjects, but the reason I'm telling you this story is because he shared with me some beliefs that were so close to the truth but weren't quite there.

He believed, for example, that the earth had a soul. It was a surprisingly close guess at the existence of Gaia, albeit nestled into his own worldview. He also believed that the planets were being pushed by the motivating force of the sun, which he equated to God. He was so close! Newton's theories regarding gravity hadn't come out yet—and Newton based some of his work on Kepler's Laws of Planetary Motion—but it was fascinating to see Kepler piecing things together with incomplete information and faith.

And then he told me something that struck me profoundly. He said that he was seeking "harmony," which to him meant some mystical connection between numerology, the movement of the stars and planets, mathematics, and even music. The connection between all things existed, he believed, but we were simply as yet unable to perceive it.

I was so tempted to give him magical sight so that he could see that everything *was* connected, but of course that would have been irresponsible and even dangerous for me to do at that point. But I agreed with him and encouraged him to keep pursuing his interests, because even without accurate information, he was nearing some revelations. I paid for his drinks and said, "May harmony find you," which became a sort of blessing I've bestowed on people ever since.

Kepler published his first two laws of planetary motion eight years later, and ten years after that added the third. They've held up to this day. He also is considered the father of modern optics and more, and all this while being pushed and pulled in different directions by competing ideologies and priorities.

Some in his position may have given up, but not Johannes Kepler. He sought harmony, to reconcile what couldn't be reconciled, and in his efforts made more progress toward the truth than most humans ever achieve.

"All of which is to say, Oberon and Starbuck, that you can find out certain truths—like which sausage is best—if you persistently seek it out. Approach it methodically, scientifically, and analyze your data, and you will arrive at an answer, even if it takes you years, as it took Kepler."

Well. Ho hooooo! Rarely have I ever been so inspired. Starbuck and I looked at each other through clouds of soapy bubbles and knew that we had been given the quest of a lifetime.

<Atticus, I would like to request an inspirational poster of Johannes Kepler to remind us that we can discover the scientific truth of things if we are patient and diligent.>

<The truth of sausage!> Starbuck said. <Yes food!>

"I'll see what I can do," Atticus said.

<Think of it, Starbuck. I've believed for many years that chicken apple is the best, but what if it isn't? It might be close—like Kepler thought the sun moved the planets with the force of God when it was really just gravity—but there might be some other sausage that's best and we need to find it! Or else confirm that I'm correct about the chicken apple. Either way, it is our duty to seek the truth! For science!>

<Tasty, delicious science!> my Boston terrier buddy cheered.

We got out of the bath and waited impatiently for Atticus to give us a quick towel dry before we zoomed out of house, more excited than we've been in thirteen centuries.

Atticus was right. Having choices is a blessing, and the tension between them can lead us to revelation if we are open to it. Starbuck and I choose to seek the finest sausage in the world, and when are successful however many years in the future, then harmony will find us.

A RIOTOUS DISTRACTION

You know how sometimes you eat a thing and it's so dang good going down, but you pay for it later on the backside? That happened to Starbuck recently. I don't know what he ate, but it came out unusually sticky and he had, shall we say, *remnants* hanging around. Which I didn't notice at first but he certainly felt, because he said something about it to me.

<Oberon, will you do me a favor and inspect my ass? Do I have any dingleberries there?>

Normally I do not enjoy dingleberry inspection but because Starbuck is a friend, I looked and confirmed that he had issues.

<I suggest you go outside and do some butt wheelies in the grass,> I said. <If you do it in here on the carpet, Rose will summon a lightning bolt and obliterate you from the earth.>

Starbuck's already round eyes boggled. <She can do that?>

<Not yet. But I think she would spontaneously manifest the powers of a wizard if she saw a wheelie track in her house.>

<Okay. Come with me and see if I do this right!>

He darted out of the house through the doggie door and I followed with eagerness because honestly, I don't care who you are, butt wheelies are pretty fun to watch.

Starbuck hit the grass and started skidding his dump truck with gusto.

<Attaboy!> I told him. <You show those berries!>

After he made a pass he got up, scooted over to me, and turned around to facilitate another inspection. <Did I get them all?>

<Almost! I said. <There is one left on the right side. Go again!>

He went again and really worked that right side, which I found immensely entertaining. When he returned for a spot check he was all clean, but I lied and told him to go one more time. He was panting after that and I'd had my fun, so I told him he was good.

<Thanks, Oberon, he said. <I owe you one.>

For some reason, that caused Atticus to interrupt from inside the house. He'd overheard our mental conversation.

Hold up, his voice said in our heads. *Why do you owe him one, Starbuck? I missed the beginning of whatever this is.*

When we explained, he stated that Starbuck didn't owe me anything and ordered us into the house and into the bathtub.

<Both of us at the same time?> I said.

Yes. I have a story for both of you. This is a teachable moment. One we were in the tub and he'd got the bubbles in there, he told us to pay attention.

There are favors and then there are *favors*. The most dangerous kind are the favors to be named later. The person who comes to collect will never do so at a convenient time, and it will never be a small matter. But sometimes, chains of favors get called in because a person who owes someone also has someone who owes him, and he passes the buck to make sure the unpleasantness doesn't fall to him.

I was lounging in a rooftop hot tub in Singapore in 1922 when the Morrigan found me. I owed her more favors than I could ever repay and she knew it. Somehow, someone she owed needed a favor in New York City and she didn't want to do it.

"It involves members of organized crime," she explained in her throaty death rasp as she slipped into the hot water with me.

"Surely you can handle them?"

"In combat? Without question, Siodhachan. But combat is not called for. Discretion and tact are indicated and those are not my traditional strengths. They are members of the patriarchy who objectify women and will not pay me my due respect. If I talk to them for any length of time, I will kill them and thereby fail to honor what is owed. So you will go to New York for me and meet with these men and do what needs to be done. You will honor a debt to me, and I will honor my debt at the same time."

"May I ask to whom you owe this debt?"

"You may not. But they have also passed this on to me as I am passing it on to you."

I snorted. "How terrible is this favor that it's being passed along so much? Do they want me to murder children or something?"

"I think not. The favor itself is not so onerous. It's more the enduring stain of associating with such men that we are trying to avoid."

"So it's okay to stain me?"

"You are so stained already that one more will not make any appreciable difference."

"Fair enough. Will you at least transport me there, to hide my passage from Aenghus Óg?"

"Yes, I will do that much."

She escorted me through the planes from Singapore to New York, and my first stop was at a tailor to update my wardrobe to blend in. It was nearing the middle of September, and when it came to haberdashery, the tailor recommended a felt hat, as Felt Hat Day, September 15, was fast approaching. If I wore a straw hat at that point, people would knock it off my head and stomp on it.

This was no formal holiday but a social norm of the time: light summer hats made of straw could no longer be worn after the fifteenth without suffering widespread ridicule and risking a mild assault. I took his advice and went with the felt hat, even though I hoped not to remain in New York all that long.

I didn't realize it at the time, but it was the year of *The Great Gatsby*. In F. Scott Fitzgerald's novel, Gatsby had been throwing lavish parties all summer in hopes of attracting his crush, Daisy Buchanan. It was a thorough criticism of the rich and careless that most Americans would wind up reading in high school, but rather than absorbing the lesson that obscenely rich people hurt others and maybe they shouldn't have the power to do that, everyone just wanted to be rich.

During this time in America, alcohol had been outlawed–they called it Prohibition. It meant that organized crime figures made plenty of money by bootlegging in addition to their other pursuits. Bars were hidden from public view and you had to know where to find them and speak a password to get in. These places were called speakeasies. I was supposed to meet two men at the back of Ratner's on Manhattan's lower east side, a speakeasy that still exists today, in fact, though now it's simply called The Back Room. You had to pass through a gate and descend a short flight of steps that led to a tunnel between two buildings, only to emerge into a courtyard with a flight of steps you took up to the speakeasy.

I'd been given the password, a description of the contacts, and a reference. The rest was up to me. I went in just wearing my suit, no sword, with a showy money clip in my pocket to give me some legitimacy as a criminal. The suit was gray and not my favorite–but it was an off-the-rack thing the tailor had ready, with a blue shirt and paisley tie and a matching gray trilby hat. I couldn't exactly disguise my red hair, but I did visit the barber to get it trimmed and styled in something horrifically lubed to complete my disguise as a modern New Yorker.

The speakeasy had wood floors with large red throw rugs on them and red plush upholstery on the couches and chairs. There was a red brick fireplace blazing merrily away it bathed the room in an orange glow, reflected by the hammered brass tiles on the ceiling. Paintings on the walls featured nudes, and cocktails were served in teacups. I ordered a Bee's Knees and asked where I could find Bugsy and Lucky. The bartender's eyes flicked to a tough guy standing next to me and he said, "Who wants to know?"

"I'm the guy that's been sent to do them a favor. They should be expecting me."

"What's your name?"

"Sean Thornton," I said, a throwaway name that coincidentally matched that of a character John Wayne would play thirty years later in a 1952 movie called *The Quiet Man*.

"Wait here."

I waited and sipped my drink and eventually the man returned.

"I gotta search you for weapons first, then I'll take you back."

His thick fingers patted me down while I patiently endured the indignity. He found my money clip, which I pointed out was not a weapon, and returned it. Once satisfied, he led me to a bookcase, knocked twice, and opened it, revealing a back room for VIPs. Inside there were six men in suits sitting around a table with empty teacups and full ashtrays and three women in flapper dresses who had draped themselves languorously over some of the men.

Everyone checked me out, but two men eyed me intensely. One wore a pale blue suit and another wore charcoal, which matched his eyes and hair.

"You're the guy? Sean Thornton?" Charcoal asked.

"I'm the guy. Someone called in a favor and I'm the one who's supposed to make sure it gets done. You are…?"

"They call me Lucky Luciano. This here's Bugsy Siegel." Their names meant nothing to me at the time, but I learned later that they were major figures in organized crime. Bugsy Siegel, in particular, was a very violent man who had already killed a number of people and would kill many more. He would eventually leave New York and become instrumental in developing the Las Vegas Strip. Lucky Luciano rose to become the head of the Genovese crime family and the head of the National Crime Syndicate. They had no way of knowing, of course, of my own storied past.

"How can I help?"

"Hold on, slow down a little bit," Lucky said. "You Irish mob?"

"Irish, yes. Mob, no. I'm independent."

"Independent what?"

"Whatever you need."

Bugsy spoke for the first time. "Hits?"

"Normally organizations have their own people for that and it's much more cost effective. I'm expensive."

Siegel's eyes scanned me again, his disbelief plain. "You're that good?"

"I'm the guy who gets called in for favors. Those are more precious than money, as you well know. Now. What can I do for you?"

The two mobsters exchanged a glance and gave each other a tiny nod, then Lucky turned to the other people present. "Give us the room, please."

It took a minute for the men and women to disentangle themselves and exit the room, but once the bookcase door was shut, I was invited to sit. Siegel watched me move, a predator who was always thinking how best to take you down. Luciano did most of the talking.

"We need a distraction on Mulberry Street tomorrow, the stretch of it that borders Columbus Park, a bit after five o'clock. Basically, a riot. One that lasts for a while and doesn't cause a lot of property damage."

"Could it be contained to the park?"

"It could spread through there but should not be contained to the park. We need it up and down the street, causing a distraction, fouling traffic, occupying cops."

"I see. Are you looking for fatalities?"

"No. I mean, we don't actually care about that. If it happens, fine. It's not a requirement. We just want the distraction, and we can't spare the men to start something like that. We'll be busy with something else. Can you do it?"

"Absolutely."

I had no idea how I would do that, but figured I had a day to come up with something.

"How?" Bugsy asked. He wasn't going to let that part slide. He seemed to enjoy coming in hot with specific questions.

"Won't know until I scout the area. But you will have a distraction tomorrow just after five o'clock. And after that, the favor is paid in full."

"It better be good."

"With only a day to prepare, it won't exactly be Homeric. But it'll get the job done."

"If you do this right, we could have other jobs for you," Luciano said.

"Thank you, but I prize my independence. I'll be leaving New York in any case, as my services are already engaged elsewhere."

That last part was a lie, but I didn't want them to think they could use me again or that I'd be used by their competition. Safest for me if they accepted now that I was a one-time contractor.

They regarded me in silence for a while until Luciano eventually tapped the table. "Okay."

I never asked them what they would be busy doing during that distraction. Not relevant to my job. They might have been planning a heist or a murder or both—not my business. But I did feel sullied by association, knowing that by carrying out their wishes I was complicit in whatever they had planned. That is the true danger of owing favors: You get drawn into situations you would never voluntarily participate in because someone has leverage over you.

I left the speakeasy and walked over to Columbus Park, spending a decent amount of time simply watching people pass by on Mulberry Street. There were teenagers out in midafternoon, free from school and any semblance of good manners. One of them, unprompted, called me a goofy ginger bastard, but that was more than a hundred years ago and he's dead now, so ha ha.

At five o'clock the character of the street changed. The factories vomited up scads of workers going home, as well as the docks not far to the south, and Mulberry Street became quite busy as throngs of people thinking of dinner tried to navigate their way through the crush. And what was super noticeable at the time was that almost everyone wore a hat–it's not a necessary part of fashion now, but back then, they were ubiquitous. I knew exactly what to do.

The next day was September 13. I had gone to a bank and changed my money into fives–quite a lot of money back then, especially for a teenager. I distributed them liberally among the local teens once they emerged from school and told them at five o'clock it was time to pretend it was Felt Hat Day. "It's coming two days earlier this year, if you know what I mean. Find those straw hats and destroy them."

They didn't question my motivations or whether this was, in fact, a good idea. It was exactly the kind of small-scale mayhem and petty cruelty that they enjoyed. I was rewarding them for what was already in their hearts.

So once five o'clock rolled around, I got my riot. Teens went up and down Mulberry Street, knocking the straw hats off every man they saw wearing one and stomping on it. Some of them objected and brawls started and it simply escalated from there. The Straw

Hat Riots of 1922 were my fault, and I did it to provide cover for whatever Bugsy Siegel and Lucky Luciano wanted to do that day. The riots went on for a few more days after that, the teenagers needing no further encouragement to piss off the populace, but by that time I was already back in Singapore, lounging in my hot tub and mourning my disastrous haircut.

Returning that favor cost me time, money, and a messed-up do that took me months to regrow. Not to mention a lingering sense of guilt over helping mobsters accomplish something. But it wasn't that bad, honestly, as far as favors go. I've had to do far worse in service to a debt. My ill-fated trip to Asgard to honor a debt to Leif Helgarson comes to mind.

"So I think," Atticus said, "you two should do a kindness for one another as often as you think of them. But favors are to be avoided. They are leverage—a power imbalance—and that can lead to problems great and small."

Starbuck tilted his head to one side. <So I should ask Oberon to do me a kindness instead of a favor?>

"Correct."

My Boston terrier buddy looked up at me. <Oberon, when we get out of the tub, will you do me a kindness and go zoom with me in the backyard?>

<Only if you will be so kind as to zoom with me!> I said.

We agreed it was good to be kind and had a most excellent zoom together after our bathtime. Atticus really did us a favor there.

THE MAN WHO DODGED THE GUILLOTINE

Starbuck and I had our first real argument, and it was over a woman who may or may not exist named Patricia. I maintained that she does not exist, and Starbuck insisted that she does.

<Sausage Patty is real!> he said.

<She can't be real, because that would mean Cow Patty is also real, and we both know she isn't, so because there is no Cow Patty, there is no Sausage Patty! You have simply taken a delicious breakfast food and improperly turned it into a proper noun!>

<There is nothing improper about Sausage Patty! She is the greatest good! She gives us sausage and that's it! No downsides! I pray to her for sausage and then I get sausage! That is how a goddess should work!>

<A goddess? I've already written *The Dead Flea Scrolls*. That is the religion for dogs! Be Sirius!>

<Atticus read *The Dead Flea Scrolls* to me and parts of it are sad! There is nothing sad about Sausage Patty!>

That got my hackles up and I growled. <You can't have a belief system that doesn't grapple with the existence of evil!>

Starbuck barked, <Yes I can! My system with Sausage Patty works perfectly! I believe I should have sausage and she agrees! We are both happy!>

<There is more to life than sausage!> I shouted, but then I staggered back and sat down because I couldn't believe I just said that. I had rocked my own world.

<What! You are a mad dog! Next you'll probably say you quite like squirrels!>

That brought me back to boiling because that was the worst insult I could imagine. <I would never! You take that back!>

<No squirrels!>

<*Of course* no squirrels! I never suggested otherwise! I wrote a whole scroll about the evil of squirrels!>

Atticus overheard our mental shouting and came outside to investigate, because we were having our throwdown in the backyard. It was a rather nice day out and it was a shame that we were ruining it with a fight. He discovered us squared up and growling at each other.

"Hey, hey, calm down, you two. Whatever this is about, I promise it's not as big a deal as you're making it. There's no need for two friends to be this angry with each other."

We each took turns airing our grievances and Atticus pointed out to me that if Starbuck wanted to believe in something I didn't, we could still be friends because we still shared many values in common—a dislike of squirrels, a love for sausage, and the joy of urinating on fire hydrants, for example.

"If I fought with everyone who doesn't believe the same things I do, I'd have no friends at all," he said. "For centuries, I was the only person in the world worshipping the pagan Irish deities the way they used to be. Now Owen is doing it too, but still, that means everyone else in the world believes something different, and that's okay. One of the worst ideas out there is the one that says your morality must come from a faith. But people of many faiths have turned out to be cruel, just as people with no faith have managed to live virtuous lives that harm no one. Someone's faith–or lack of it–is not a good indicator of their moral character."

<What is a good indicator?> I asked.

"Whether they want to help people or exploit them is often a good clue."

<Do I help people?>

"You help me all the time. You keep me focused on the present and warn me of danger, and so does Starbuck. Plus you make me laugh, which is a gift."

<Sausage is a gift.>

"That is true. Listen, you're not particularly dirty at the moment, but I want to tell you a story and wash away the bad vibes. So let's have you both hop in the tub and I'll sling you a tale of a guy who loved an empress, snuck out of a country in disguise, and frustrated one of the biggest colonial powers in the world."

Starbuck and I scrambled into the bathroom to hear all about him.

Francisco de Miranda was born to wealthy parents in the back half of the eighteenth century and grew up in Venezuela, which was under Spanish colonial rule at the time. His connections afforded him a good education and a trip to Madrid, where he studied languages and got himself a commission in the Spanish army. He got deployed to northern Africa, defending a colonial outpost there that reminded him uncomfortably of such facilities and practices in Venezuela. After that he was sent to Cuba as the Spanish entered the American Revolutionary war on the side of the Americans–Spain wanted to sock it to the British if they could, as did France. He participated in the siege of Pensacola and also the capture of the Bahamas.

That Bahamas episode, however, got him arrested by a Spanish commander, Bernardo de Gálvez, who was really mad at Miranda's superior officer, and Miranda pretty much decided then that Spanish colonialism was bullshit, and he had the United States as shining recent example of what could happen when you threw off colonial rule. He got out of prison but heard the Spanish Inquisition was coming for him, so he basically abandoned the colonizers, kissing his career in the Spanish hierarchy goodbye forever, and went into exile in the United States. He met Thomas Jefferson, Alexander Hamilton, and George Washington, getting ideas from the guys who successfully threw off the yoke of their oppressors, and began openly talking about how South American colonies could win their independence from Spain. That just made the Inquisition want him even more–but you see, Francisco de Miranda was the one guy who *always* expected the Spanish Inquisition. He dodged them for years.

How? Partially by being a very charming and accomplished lover. Wherever he went in the US and Europe, he had a series of super-hot affairs with wealthy and powerful women. How powerful? Try

Catherine the Great, Empress of Russia. She liked him so much that she gave him a Russian passport and diplomatic immunity, which prevented the Spanish from having him arrested and extradited in several other countries he visited. So he was able to travel throughout Europe and doors opened to him in every palace because he had talked with or slept with many of the most powerful people on the planet, and once he got into the ears of these kings and queens he told them that the people of South America deserved to be free because the Spanish were legendary assholes. And anyone living at that time who had heard of the Inquisition found it easy to agree.

Miranda said a lot more than that, of course, and his words were very well received. Not enough to get material support for a revolution, but well enough to isolate Spain so that they wouldn't get any help from other countries if their colonies rebelled. And honestly that was a huge deal: His diplomatic efforts laid the groundwork for eventual independence movement led by Simón Bolívar. In Latin America he is now known as the Precursor, whereas Bolívar is the Liberator; Miranda's work abroad made Bolívar's revolution possible.

Miranda was not the only person in the world to be inspired by America's revolution. Plenty of the French admired it too. They decided to have their own revolution, and since Miranda was in favor of people overthrowing monarchies, he joined the revolutionaries as a general in their armies. His name is engraved on the Arc de Triomphe in Paris because of his contributions. This annoyed some of the same monarchies that had supported him before, and he definitely burned some bridges there, but he also ran afoul of the French he was helping, as almost everyone did in those days: He was arrested during the Reign of Terror as a traitor because one of his military campaigns on their behalf had not been successful.

This was where I came to see him—not meet him. I was in Paris during the Reign of Terror because I was learning a lot about how good ideas can go bad and just keep getting worse. Like a loaf of bread that gets forgotten—it's just politely moldy after a few days, but then the rot really sets in and it's hopeless. That's what was happening in France. It was a great idea to live without a monarchy and aristocracy because those are absolutely terrible, but the methods employed to achieve that were horrific and the goalposts shifted so rapidly that the Committee for Public Safety was basically arresting anyone who disagreed with them or hurt their feelings a little bit.

Miranda was one of the very few people able to successfully argue himself out of execution during the Reign of Terror; I was there for that. He got arrested again later on and was held in prison for a while, and that taught him to consider that while revolutions might seem like a smashing good idea, the deployment and establishment of a new government makes all the difference.

He avoided the guillotine again and was set free, but the thrill was gone now; he was thinking maybe the revolutionary government wasn't so hot. Before he could be arrested on yet another petty charge, he snuck out of France in a disguise and made his way back to England and eventually the United States once more, where he continued to tell everyone that the Spanish were terrible and deserved to be kicked out of the western hemisphere.

Thomas Jefferson and James Madison listened to him and wouldn't let the United States get involved, but promised they wouldn't interfere either if Miranda wanted to start something. He got enough backing from a wealthy businessman to mount a minor invasion of Venezuela, but it didn't do much except piss off the Spanish even more. He wound up traveling back to England, continuing his agitation and incidentally getting married and producing a couple of kids, and in 1811 an opportunity arose for him to return to Venezuela. Simón Bolívar and others had deposed the colonial rulers of Venezuela in 1810, and they were seeking British recognition and financial aid to cement their independence from Spain. They also met with Miranda and asked him to come back and be a part of the new government.

He agreed and eventually led the First Venezuelan Republic; they even adopted the flag design he'd come up with when he'd mounted his ill-fated invasion a few years earlier.

But the new republic suffered from some of the same pressures the young United States did: Many of the people living there were still loyal to the Spanish monarchy. The United States successfully suppressed or expelled most British loyalists–they were pretty brutal about it, and many of them moved to Canada. But Venezuela had trouble doing the same, and economic pressures plus a massive earthquake doomed the fledgling government before it could consolidate its strength. The republic deteriorated and the royalists occupied larger and larger chunks of the country until Miranda recognized all was lost. Was he qualified to recognize that?

Absolutely. Keep in mind he'd been a military leader for decades and a keen observer of colonial politics his entire life. He wound up signing an armistice with the royalists, which Bolivar considered to be treasonous. So what did Bolívar do? He handed Miranda over to the royalists, and he was shipped off to a Spanish prison after successfully dodging the Inquisition all that time.

Was Miranda—a man who'd dedicated the majority of his life to Venezuelan independence—a traitor? Lots of people had trouble buying that, and while Bolívar is recognized as being the Liberator, his decision to betray Miranda is considered a stain on his record.

I never met Bolívar, and I'm sure signing an armistice may have seemed to him like a betrayal on Miranda's part. But the military and political reality of the time was clear: the armistice was the best way out of an impossible situation. Handing over a man who'd fought tirelessly for Venezuela—and who'd come back to it at Bolivar's request!—was absolutely a betrayal. How could Bolívar forget the many values he and Miranda shared? That is what I would like to know. But it's a pattern I see again and again: people who should be the best of friends sometimes turn on one another over a disagreement that should not determine either's fate. But Miranda died in a Spanish prison because of Bolívar.

He lived an extraordinary life and may have accomplished even more if he'd not been betrayed at the end.

"So that is why I am very concerned that you two may let a minor disagreement swell up into something huge," Atticus said as he rinsed us down and toweled us dry. "Holy wars are ridiculous. Just love food and belly rubs and ass sniffing and your many other shared interests, like zoomies after baths, okay?"

We agreed to this and zoomed out of there and loved it.

<Hey, I'm sorry I got upset about Sausage Patty,> I told Starbuck as we took a sharp turn in the backyard. <It's good that you have a thing that makes you happy.>

<I'm sorry I said you might like squirrels,> Starbuck replied. <That was mean.>

<Atticus said I help him live in the present. We should presently ask him to buy us a present of sausage from that butcher shop with the thousands of varieties. That would be super helpful of us.>

<I present to you English: It's absurd,> Starbuck said. <But also yes, we should do that.>

There sure is a lot to get mad about if you go looking for it. Squirrels are everywhere, after all. But there's a lot to be happy about too if you look for that instead. I see plenty to be happy about with my Druid and Boston terrier buddy.

Squirrels persist, but so do I.

ACKNOWLEDGEMENTS

I must first thank the paid subscribers to my newsletter, Words & Birds, because they basically made this possible. Short stories are not, in general, a worthwhile endeavor for authors because they can buy maybe three tacos for what they get paid and the time spent vs. tacos-earned ratio is fairly dire. This is why you don't see a lot of short story collections; they simply aren't worth it to authors who need to eat.

The thing is: Short stories can be *fun*. These were especially fun because I got the opportunity to finish up some old loose ends from the novels I never could address (like the Triple Nonfat Double Bacon Five-Cheese Mocha) without getting sidetracked from the larger narrative.

So again, I am turbo grateful to my subscribers for making this possible; their collective financial support bought enough tacos to make this project happen–it would *not* have happened without them. So thanks, y'all. (I'm now working on a new collection of Iron Druid short stories. If you'd like to buy me one taco per month in exchange for a story–a bargain, I say!–you can do so at wordsandbirds.ink.)

Thanks to K.C. Alexander and Jason Hough and all the Seattle peeps for encouragement; Chuck Wendig and Delilah S. Dawson for stocking me up with sanity points; Phineas X. Jones for awesome cover art; and Luke Daniels for outstanding audiobook narration.

Mega thanks also to my Canadian writing peeps,

who often throw down words with me at this coffee shop or that: Kate Heartfield, Amal El-Mohtar and Stu West, Derek Kunsken, Brandon Crilly, Erin Rockfort, Marie Bilodeau, Lydia Hawke, Evan May, Marco Cultrera, Craig Shackleton, Claudie Arsenault, Cortni Fernandez, Nathan Burgoine, Tyler Goodier, and Nicole Lavigne.

Thanks also to my family for the love, and of course, thank you to everyone I've ever met who's had a dog for me to pet. Dogs are the best and they deserve a snack.

SAUSAGE CREDITS

We must acknowledge that nothing is possible without sausage. Its rich and variegated flavors are manifold and require recognition as they provided vital fuel and inspiration for these stories.

Standard breakfast patties were most often consumed, but there were also numerous sausages secured from a Quebecois saucissier including whiskey bacon cheese, Andouille, pesto and bocconcini, lime and coriander, Chipolata, and Weisswurst, along with special guest sausages like Schueblig, Acupulco, Merguez, Toulouse, and Provencal Duck.

ABOUT THE AUTHOR

Kevin Hearne is the *New York Times* bestselling author of the Iron Druid Chronicles, the Ink & Sigil series, the Seven Kennings trilogy, and co-author of the Tales of Pell with Delilah S. Dawson. He's into nature photography, heavy metal, and beard maintenance. He loves planning road trips and sometimes even takes them.

Website: kevinhearne.com
Bluesky: @kevinhearne.bsky.social
Instagram/Threads: @kevinhearne

www.ingramcontent.com/pod-product-compliance
Lightning Source LLC
Chambersburg PA
CBHW061216080425
24778CB00012B/706